SMALL TOWN LOVE

BOOK 1 IN THE LOVETOWN SERIES

MICHELLE STIMPSON
MICHELLE LINDO-RICE

Michelle Stimpson
P.O. Box 1592
Cedar Hill, TX 75106-1592

Michelle Lindo-Rice
386 Walmart Drive
Suite 7 PMB 80
Camden DE 19934

Edited by Michelle Chester, http://www.ebm-services.com, and Felecia Murrell, http://www.yzcounsel.com.
Cover design by Oasis Sites - order@oasissites.com.

ACKNOWLEDGMENTS

From *Michelle Lindo-Rice:*

A big thank you to Michelle Stimpson for suggesting this joint venture. Kisses and hugs to my family and my wonderful husband. Thank you, John, for designing our book covers for the Lovetown series. A special thank you to my beta reader, Fran Purnell, for the advice and feedback, and to my reviewers.

Sincerely,
Michelle Lindo-Rice
www.michellelindorice.com

From *Michelle Stimpson:*
I continue to be amazed at God's goodness. It never gets old. I'm so thankful for my family's continued support and to the readers who keep me on their bookshelves!
Special thanks to my son, Steven, for giving me some "young man" advice.
Thanks, Michelle Lindo-Rice, for jumping into this with me. It's such a pleasure working with you and so sweet to see your love with John blossom!

Blessings!
Michelle Stimpson
www.MichelleStimpson.com

Michelle Lindo-Rice's books

TELL ME LIES

"One of the things I love about Author Lindo-Rice's writing style is her ability to capture the true essence of her characters without them being over the top. The characters and the situations they encounter are relatable and always leaves the reader to ponder on ways they can better their lives."

– Orsayor Simmons, Book Referees

SILENT PRAISE

"Michelle Lindo-Rice's *Silent Praise*, Able to Love book three, has at its core a Christian inspirational message, by way of a very enjoyable romance ... The horror and disappointment are realistically written with great visual and sensory scenes that immediately pulled me in and held me in place to the end in one sitting."

—Michelle Monkou, *Special Edition of USA Today – HEA*

WHAT READERS ARE SAYING ABOUT:

Michelle Stimpson's books

BOAZ BROWN

...this thought-provoking tale of anger, prejudice and romance offers important lessons for all.

-Publishers Weekly

JOY FOR THE JOURNEY

It felt like a family reunion being able to catch up on everyone's lives. It had so many upheavals that was both positive and negative. So worth waiting for and the bonus painting was a welcome surprise and an unexpected bonus.

-Amazon Reviewer

DEDICATION

For everyone who still believes in love.

PROLOGUE

Sean knocked on the screen door of his best friend, Jhavon's grandmother's house and opened it at the same time. If they lived in a larger town, maybe Big would have kept her front door locked. But here, in Lovetown, Texas, there wasn't a need. Somebody next door or across the street would have already registered Sean's presence on King Drive.

"What up?" Sean announced himself to the household that might as well have been his, given how much time he spent there.

"Big is sleep." Jazmin, "Jazzy" fussed at a volume almost higher than Sean's greeting. She didn't even look up at him as she walked through the living room to the bedroom she shared with her identical twin sister, Janiyah.

Niya.

He hadn't seen her yet, but he could smell her sweet

scent in the small house. Maybe it was roses. Maybe it was strawberries. Maybe it was his imagination that, over the past months, was wild with thoughts of her.

He had known Niya for most of his life because he had been friends with Jhavon since preschool. Head Start, in fact. The government-run school for low-income children, though it hadn't occurred to Sean, Jhavon, or any of their friends they were "low-income." They were just kids having fun, learning, living their lives.

Back then, Sean had a mom and a dad and some good memories. But when his mother left, a piece of Sean's happiness went with her. His father's happiness slipped away, too. And, all of a sudden, Sean found himself hanging out with Jhavon's family more and more.

Jhavon's mom would make a cake for no reason at all. "Just wanted something sweet," she'd say in her chirpy, bird-like voice.

She would let the four of them—Sean, Jhavon, Jazzy, and Niya—lick the batter bowl with their fingers. Vying for the last few fingers full of flavor, their four heads would bump one another. "Stop hogging it all!" and "Don't use your *whole* hand!" they'd yell at one another.

And then Jhavon and the twins' parents died. Both of them. Like, boom-boom. Sean was too young to measure the time surrounding their deaths in years or months. He had processed them in feelings. Worse, and worse still. And before they knew it, Jhavon and Sean started feeling like all they had was each other. Like brothers.

Which was what made Sean's secret crush on Niya difficult. This girl—no, she was all woman now with curves and lips and perfume and hoop earrings, though he couldn't recall the exact moment it happened. Like the terrible memories, the good ones of Niya followed a progression—cute, beautiful, amazing. She'd been cute the night she went to the Junior High prom. She'd been beautiful that time he'd seen her at the Lovetown vs. Red Valley homecoming football game. She'd been so breathtaking, surpassing the bougie Red Valley girls from the right side of the tracks. Sean had done a double-take and the girl he'd taken to the game had slapped his shoulder for looking at another female.

And tonight, he saw her as "amazing." Jazzy was trying her hair-braiding skills on Niya. "If I can figure out how to braid hair, I'll be ballin' for real in this little bitty town."

Big woke up from her nap for a few hours, made beef ribs, green beans, and mashed potatoes with gravy, and went back to bed. Everyone else stayed up watching movies. Sean couldn't remember what they were watching because the screen's glow on Niya's face was all he wanted to see. She tilted her head this way and that, allowing Jazzy to part and braid, add a swath of fake hair to her shoulder length curls, unbraid, and start over again.

Niya had been so patient. So encouraging. "Come on, sis. You can do this."

And all the while, Niya had been the one who saw the "surprise" ending of the movie coming in the film a full hour before it happened.

"How did you know he was going to find the money?" Jhavon had asked when whatever it was did occur in the plot.

"Niya probably watched this movie already," Jazzy teased.

"I did not," Niya insisted. "Don't hate on me because I'm brilliant."

At that, they had all laughed, even Niya. And it occurred to him, then, that this was why he had fallen for her instead of Jazzy. Niya could be feisty when she needed to be. She was smart. And she let her sister try for hours and hours despite what appeared to be painful tugging at the hair on Niya's scalp. Plus the fact that her smooth, brown legs, twisted in all different directions depending on Jazzy's braiding angle, went on for days.

He couldn't keep this level of admiration to himself much longer. And, if Sean wasn't mistaken, Niya felt it, too. She'd averted her eyes from his and shied away from his stolen glances but she couldn't hide her smile. It was a miracle Jhavon hadn't seen the chemistry sizzling between them.

"Whatchu wanna watch next?" Jhavon asked when the credits rolled for the first movie.

"I've got an old one in mind," Niya said. She cleared her throat. "*The Lion King.*"

Jazzy scoffed, "*The Lion King*? No way."

"Ummm...I don't think so," Jhavon said, shaking his head.

Sean raised his hand. "I vote for *The Lion King*, too. I

mean, think about it. Scar. Mufasa. Simba. How can you deny—"

"Anck." Jazzy buzzed him out. "We are way too old to be watching a cartoon."

Sean shook his head. He looked down at Niya, whose eyes fluttered up at him. *There*. He'd seen it. The spark in her eyes, again.

And, in that moment, Sean looked over at Jhavon. He must have seen what transpired, because his mouth hung open and his eyes widened with shock before they narrowed to slits.

"Pick something else," Jazzy said, "*Not* a cartoon," unaware of Sean and Jhavon's silent communication.

Jhavon hopped up onto his feet. "Hey. Me and Sean are going to run to the store and get a few things, all right? Y'all figure out the movie. We'll be right back."

Sean didn't protest. He was kind of hungry and could use a snack. Even more, he could use a moment alone with Jhavon. Because it was only a matter of time before something popped off between him and Niya and Sean needed Jhavon to be cool with it.

Unfortunately, Sean would never get that chance.

1

NIYA

I should have been happy the day I turned 27, but I wasn't. I was only three years away from 30, the age my mother died, an age my father and my brother, Jhavon, never reached.

My grandma, Big, said people in our family died young. "We got a hex on us," she told me and my twin sister, Jazmin, as we were walking from Jhavon's grave site the day we buried him. Jazmin and I were 14 when Jhavon died and when Big whispered those words to us in her raspy, superstitious tone. We'd heard the words before, but now that Jhavon, who had been three years older, had died, the curse seemed more real than ever.

The countdown was on.

So when I woke up at 6:58 a.m. on August 3rd, my 27th birthday, anxiety gripped my neck and pinned me in bed for the first five minutes. I took several quick breaths, tightening my fists around the fitted sheet. *Only three years left.*

I remembered one summer when we visited my Uncle Poe in Oklahoma, he took us to church, and our teacher said Jesus was 33 when He died. At the time, I thought Jesus had lived to a ripe old age.

Not so anymore.

Sunlight still managed to stream through the dingy window, making the blackened walls appear dirtier than ever. I had tried my hardest to clean those walls once, but the bleach I put in the water stripped the paint and Big popped me with a belt for destroying her house.

It never occurred to her or me that a fresh coat of paint might work wonders.

Lying on my bed in the small room I shared with my twin sister, Jazmin, on a lazy Sunday morning, I wondered, *How will I die?*

I wasn't even close to sick, so that was probably not how I would go. I walked or rode a bus almost everywhere I went, making a car accident unlikely. I didn't have any enemies in the neighborhood, but my neighborhood itself was a threat. Just the week before, somebody had shot up into Miss Mabel's house-store. The store part of her house had closed for a couple days.

I gotta stop going to Miss Mabel's.

With that decision made, I breathed a little easier. I figured maybe I could plan well enough to buy myself the full three years. Maybe I could make it to thirty and a half, or thirty and nine tenths. My mind ran the calculations almost effortlessly. *Twelve months in a year...divided by ten...one point two months...times nine...ten point eight...*That meant I could make it through mid-summer of my twenty-ninth year. *But I don't want to die when it's hot outside. People might not come to my funeral.*

"Niyaaaaa?" Big hollered my name from the other side of the thin wall separating my bedroom from the living room.

Before I could take a deep breath and answer, Jazmin rushed into our room and yanked the covers off my legs and feet, sending a woosh of semi-cold air up my body.

"Get your lazy butt up. Big wants you to go to the store for her," she fussed.

"Why can't you go?"

"Cause I do everything else around here."

"No, you don't," I argued.

Jazmin shifted her weight to one hip. "Which one of us is already out of bed? And which one of us got up and cooked breakfast already?"

She had a point, though I wasn't sure if she should call getting out of bed and preparing food doing "everything." Besides, she'd have to do those things whether I was around or not. That's what she got paid to do.

"Happy birthday to you too," I said with much sarcasm, staring at my mirror image. We both had the same brown eyes, perfectly arched brows, bronze skin tone, curly hair and full, wide lips. But whereas my lips often held a smile, Jazzy's was often downturned into a frown.

Rolling her eyes, Jazzy said, "Same to you. Now, get up."

There was no use in arguing with Jazmin. Big would be on her side if I tried. Conceding, I twisted my body to a sitting position and let my feet hit the floor. "What does she want at this time of the morning?"

"Bread and cigarettes. Big's been begging for her smokes, and I'll give her one today. You can go to Miss Mabel's or, if she's acting all self-righteous today and starts giving you a hard time about buying cigarettes on a church day, go to Mr. Henderson's." She said these words like we didn't already know the drill, which annoyed me even more.

"You know I don't like going to Mr. Henderson's. You don't go there yourself." We both avoided that store for two reasons. One, Mr. Henderson could talk your ear off. There was no running in and out of the store with him. The second was Jhavon had died near Mr. Henderson's store. Going there brought back too many memories and too much sadness.

"Well, hopefully Miss Mabel won't be in one of her sanctimonious moods," Jazzy said. "She wasn't the last time I went. I guess she realized she was losing too much money trying to make us all holy."

I didn't bother telling Jazmin Ms. Mabel's house-store was off limits to me because I was doing everything possible to live well into my thirtieth year. All I said was, "Okay," because, again, there's no winning with Jazmin.

"And if you end up at Mr. Henderson's, see if he has any new books by Gina Johnson."

This last statement was almost a joke because, in truth, Jazzy would read books written by just about anybody.

I washed my face, brushed my teeth, and changed clothes with no fanfare.

When I finished getting ready, I passed through the living room. Big was sitting in her wheelchair, as usual, giving her swollen, achy legs a rest. Her eyes were glued to the small television set atop an antique entertainment center.

"Morning, Big," I said. I bent down and kissed her wrinkled cheek, hating how diabetes had sucked the strength out of the strongest woman I knew.

"Don't forget my candy bar. King size," she whispered.

"You know the doctor don't want you eating all that sugar," I reminded her. "I don't need you falling into a diabetic coma."

She rolled her eyes. "I need my candy. Besides, he ain't no real doctor. He one of them nurse practitioners. That's what the government give the poor. They save the real doctors for the folks with money."

"Ummm…I'm pretty sure practitioners know what they're talking about, too," I ventured. I slipped my feet into the flip-flops Jazmin had left on the floor next to the front door.

"Bet not let your sister see you putting on her shoes." Big winked at me.

I gave a little smile followed by a thumbs up and left the house, the screen door swinging behind me.

Big had a sense of humor left, if little else. She hadn't always been *this* poor. I mean, she'd always lived in that small, shotgun house, as far as I knew. But back when I was in elementary and junior high, Big used to sell dinners from the house, and people came from all over Lovetown, TX, to buy a plate. From businessmen in suits to prostitutes in the clothes they'd worn the night before everybody knew about Beatrice Thompson's good cooking.

Took a while, but the city health department found out about it and gave her a bunch of fines. Tax bills, too. Big said it was because they were trying to bring in a bunch of franchises and make Lovetown one of those reformed places with coffee shops, bookstores, and over-priced high-rise apartments on every corner. She said probably one of them well-to-do businessmen got wind of how much money she was making and blabbed to downtown about it because his sorry old momma's nasty, no-seasoning diner on the other side of the tracks was losing business.

I had been in seventh grade that year. Revitalizing the town might have been the original plan, but here it was fifteen years later and my walk down Clark Street showed the plan had failed. The two vacant lots where they'd torn down the old Piggly Wiggly—I'd worked there for five years after high school—and the Dollar Store hadn't been replaced by any coffeehouse. A ten-year-old sign reading, *Vote McCampbell for Mayor – Change is On the Way!* still stood high above the street light. McCampbell hadn't won the election, and the changes in the city never came to pass. The only change that registered for me was Big's lack of income. We were no longer rich-poor. Just regular-poor after that. Not much had changed in Lovetown or in my life since then.

It was still early enough in the day that the temperature was below 80 degrees. I passed Miss Mabel's house and continued to the corner to wait for a bus. In a small town like Lovetown, I could be waiting for an hour before our one Sunday bus driver decided to pull out of the chicken place and run his shift. But, I was determined to wait. Jazmin and Big would both fuss that it took me too long to go to the store and come back, but what else was new? Those two couldn't be pleased. There was no use in me trying.

I was attempting to survive to 30, which made my next move all the more ironic because statistics showed city buses safer than personal vehicles.

When Jhavon's old friend, Sean, pulled up to the curb in his Mustang, I smiled real wide because… well…because his presence reminded me of my brother.

"Hey, Niya. Where you goin'?" Sean's gapped-tooth smile always took me by surprise, as though I was seeing it for the first time every time. In fact, his entire face seemed different. Smoother. Older.

I answered his question. "To the store."

He gave me a confused expression. "Miss Mabel's?"

"No. The *real* store." I looked around to make sure no one had heard me. To our neighborhood, Miss Mabel *was* a real store, just like Big's operation had been a real take-out restaurant.

"You want a ride?"

I stepped closer to his car, getting a better view of him now that his head was blocking the sun. I hadn't seen Sean in ages. He'd joined the military after Jhavon died and had returned only a few times since then. He and Jhavon had been so close, Sean was like a second brother to me, so I normally wouldn't have hesitated to get in a car with him.

Today was different, though. Sean was different. I had always thought he was cute but now he was a sculpted hunk of a male who had outgrown his awkwardness and now exuded swag. Swag that made my breath catch, and I didn't know how to deal with that.

His dimples popped into place, messing with my heart's rhythm. "You wanna have a heat stroke?" he asked.

"Uhhh…no," I replied, aware my mouth was spreading into a much wider grin than I'd like.

"Then you'd better get in. Buses run slow on the weekend."

I shook off whatever resistance I had and took Sean up on his offer, hopping into the passenger's seat of his Mustang.

Once inside, I smelled his cologne, sultry and masculine.

Like one of the businessmen who used to come to Big's house every Friday and leave her a healthy tip. Another glance at Sean sent my pulse racing. He was *absolutely* cuter than I remembered. His vague facial structure had become chiseled, more refined. His hair was a precise crew cut, his brown eyes more confident. Not to mention his blue button-down shirt with black slacks. He could have been on the front of a magazine cover, except for the tooth-gap thing, which never looked bad on him.

"You're all dressed up," was all I could manage to say. "You got a job interview today?"

I could have kicked myself for asking such a silly question, seeing as it was Sunday. *What's wrong with me? It's only Sean.*

"No. I'm going to church."

I wanted to bark, *Church?* but I didn't want to insult him. I mumbled, "Oh, that's good."

"You want to come with me? I have to go back home to get my Bible and can swing back this way to get you?"

I rarely went inside a church for anything other than a funeral. But we had plenty of funerals in our family, so I figured me and God were even. I didn't need to come to His house because He had already taken enough people from mine. Yeah, me and God were even.

"Naw. I have to cook breakfast for Big." I swallowed my lie and sunk deeper into the seat. The occasional white lie came easy, but I realized I hated lying to Sean.

"Okay, maybe next time," he said, turning on the radio.

Sean's radio played gospel music softly, and I wondered if I had made the right decision to ride with him. *Is he in a cult?* Maybe he was trying to recruit me. Maybe they were going to offer me as a human sacrifice. *Maybe this is how I die.*

I kept my mouth shut most of the way to the store, nodding as Sean attempted to make small talk. From what I heard in the neighborhood, he was back home for good after being discharged from the military sometime in April. He'd earned some certification and was about to start a job in a nearby suburb. People said he was helping other people get jobs. Recruiting, I think. Sean had moved into his own apartment on the fancy side of town.

"That's good," I said. "That's great."

He waited outside for me to buy Big's things, then took me back home. When we arrived at Big's, I didn't wait for him to let me out of the car. I unlocked my door. "Thanks for the ride." I stepped toward the house.

"Niya. Wait."

I turned to face him, walking back to the rolled-down window of his car. "Yeah?"

"How's your family?" His eyes became shiny.

Instantly, I knew he was thinking of Jhavon and Sean was my second brother again. My heart softened. "We're fine. We all miss him." My short nails bit into the interior of Sean's cushioned door panel.

"Me, too. I still can't believe he's gone." Sean shook his head.

"Me, either," I agreed.

"Let me know if you need anything. *Anything*, Niya."

I nodded, then skittered away so Sean wouldn't see the tears streaming down my face.

2

SEAN

Goodness. She sure was wearing those jeans. An old song, Flo Rida's "Low", played in my mind. I closed my eyes and willed the image of Niya's luscious behind away.

It wasn't easy. I was a saved man but I wasn't blind.

I was also going to be late to church. But I couldn't look away. Niya reminded me of a younger version of the singer Mya with those lips, that banging body and those curls. Curls I wanted to run my hands through to see if they were as soft as I imagined.

I waited until Niya disappeared inside her house before wiping my brow, putting the car into gear, and turning the corner. I was glad she hadn't turned around to see me salivating after her like she was a sweet cup of coconut juice from Jamaica. Me and a few of my Navy friends had stopped in Ocho Rios for a few days on an island-hopping adventure.

Seeing Niya always brought me back in time. Back when I wasn't ready to be saved.

My insides churned. "You're not that kid anymore," I told myself.

I rolled up the windows, sucked in the cool air, and made my way across the train tracks into the "good" side of the town. I snorted. What a cliché. As a child, I'd lived contented on the other side not knowing the shack I'd grown up in wasn't the norm. Not knowing I could ever do better, be better. Sean Morrison had come far. Farther than my daddy predicted I would.

Just before I left for the Navy, I remembered him hollering, "You ain't worth more than bird poop," then he threw a hot pan of grits my way, hitting my brow, narrowly missing my face.

Caught up in the memory, I rubbed the corner of my brow where I'd been seared by the heat. Pop's words echoed in my ear as I stood hunched by the front door.

"If you asked me, the wrong boy died," Pop said, coming at me.

I bowled over from his harsh words and sank to the floor. I felt the heat of the grits seep through my one pair of khaki pants but refused to cry aloud.

"You're right, Pop. I should've died." I said the words because I agreed with Pop and thought they would calm him.

Instead of placating him, Pop became enraged. "You trying to be funny, boy?" He kicked my chin, drawing blood. Those days, I didn't have much incentive to fight back. I would've stayed there and allowed him to beat me, but then I saw the clock. I lunged to my feet, grabbed my backpack, and raced through the door. I didn't stop running until I was at the military recruiter's office.

Thankfully, Petty Officer Stewart hadn't asked any questions. He took in my bloody face and soiled clothes and held out his hand. I put a shaky hand in his. Then Petty Officer Stewart drew me close and hugged me. Treated me with dignity. He said, "Your country is proud to have you, Seaman."

I lifted my head and gave a little nod.

That was thirteen years ago. I wiped my tears, as choked up as I had been on that day.

I drove a few miles before pressing on the gas. My Mustang roared, appreciating the dust flying under its feet.

"Go, baby, go," I yelled, accelerating twenty miles past the posted speed limit. I loved the feel of the car under my control. Hearing William McDowell come on, I pumped up the volume, singing along to "Wrap Me in Your Arms." I whipped around the car in front of me and then another, before I saw the flashing red and blue lights.

Obediently, I slowed down and pulled to the curb.

I wasn't worried about getting pulled over in this part of town. I knew the cops on duty. I'd gone to school with Meathead Mike and Travis the Tease and I knew their secrets… just as they knew mine.

I turned off the engine and waited for the two burly men to approach.

"Where you goin' in such a hurry?" Travis asked, chewing on the ever-present straw. He'd been doing that since high school.

"Church," I said.

Travis guffawed. "You running from hell to get there?"

"You know you were going close to forty miles over?" Mike said.

I felt my eyes go wide. I knew I was speeding but didn't know I had been going that fast. "I'm trying to catch the nine o'clock service."

Travis eyed me with suspicion. "This isn't the way to your church."

"I left my Bible at home. I stopped by Niya's and got sidetracked so I wasn't trying to be late."

Mike whistled. "I can see how you'd get sidetracked by Niya. She's definitely eye candy."

I wondered what he meant by that but wasn't about to ask a question to which I didn't want to know the answer. Mike had this salacious look on his face that made my stomach clench. He was talking about Niya like she was a piece of steak.

Mike licked his lips. "Me and Niya go way back."

I cocked my head. *Was he saying he and Niya...?*

"Naw. She's too feisty for me. Jazzy is the one who might snag me into settling down," Travis said.

I couldn't hold back my chuckle. Travis had been feigning for Jazmin for years. Everybody knew she would never look his way, not even once. My eyes fell on the clock. It was a little after nine. I started up the car.

"I've got to get going. I don't want to miss praise and worship. And Pastor Moore's about to start a new series on Heroes of the Faith."

The officers stepped back. "All right. But we can't make it a habit of letting you off the hook. Pretty soon, we might be getting dash-cams in our vehicles. We'd have to issue a ticket then. But for now, go do your church thing. Repent to the Lord for speeding, this time. We'll swing by later to catch up."

I gritted my teeth to hide my agitation. What's up with people calling my relationship with God, a "church thing"? I couldn't stand that. God was my everything. If they only knew. Serving Him wasn't a *thing* for me. He was my life. But I wasn't about to argue with them and possibly end up with a speeding ticket after all and points on my license.

Travis gave a poor rendition of a salute. "Catch you later, Chief Morrison."

I cringed. "Stop with all that. I'm still Sean. I'm proud of my accomplishments but this title didn't make me into the man I am today. God did."

Travis held up a hand. "Don't start your preaching. It's too early in the morning for all of that."

I wanted to say, *There's never a bad time to talk about God,* but I didn't want to come off sounding cliché and, well, corny.

"You've come a long way from Cyber Tooth and High

Waters. You don't talk the same and you certainly don't look the same," Travis teased, though his voice held pride.

I nodded. Those old nicknames hurt. I placed a tongue between the now-smaller-sized gap between my teeth. I had had a gap so wide that kids said I must have lost a tooth in cyberspace, earning me the title, Cyber Tooth. I wasn't as bothered by High Waters because my pants never did fit me right. However, I was tall and I looked mean so nobody said it to my face. Lucky for them.

Mike chimed in. "I wish your old man was here to see you and eat his words." He spoke with a steel-edged tone.

We all fell silent.

"I've got to go," I said.

"We'll call at the end of our shift," Mike said. "It's your turn to cook."

I laughed. "Get ready for steaks and potatoes on the grill."

The men shrugged. I knew they weren't surprised. That's all the cooking I had mastered.

With a wave, I shot off toward my home. Three minutes later, I pulled into the gated apartment complex and whispered, "Thank you, God." I had been living here for about six weeks and every time I entered, I was struck by the elegance and beauty of my home. I couldn't help but praise Him for all His blessings. I chuckled to myself. Maybe Travis was right. I was turning into one of those high fallutin' church folks, as he called them.

I pressed the car alarm and entered the ritzy, newly-built

complex suited for the upper working class. I loved the blue plush couches in the lobby, the fresh flowers, and the fruit-infused water the staff kept on hand. Every time I came through the front door, I felt I was at a five-star hotel. It never got old. I didn't mind paying the monthly maintenance fees to keep the marble floors shiny and pay for the weekly socials. I flashed a smile at Wanda at the front desk and pretended I didn't see a couple sisters checking me out. I strutted toward the elevator, proud to be a successful black man who had defied all the stereotypes despite his upbringing.

I had God. I had a career. I had more money than I could spend. I had a home. There was only one thing missing.

A wife.

Niya's face flashed before me. This time, her lips were ruby red. I pushed that out of my mind and hummed a gospel tune to center my mind on God. I entered my apartment and took off my shoes before sinking my feet into the plush white carpet. I traipsed into my master suite and grabbed my Bible off my bed.

Twenty minutes later, I entered The Great Hope Deliverance Center. Sis. Charlene already had the church on its feet with her singing gift. It was hot and crowded, but I wasn't bothered. I finagled my way through the crowd until I was in the front row at the left corner. I nodded at the keyboard player before closing my eyes and lifting my hands in worship along with the congregation.

I don't know how long I stood there lost in His presence before I felt a consistent tug on my right leg.

I opened my eyes and looked down toward the pesky interloper of my time with God. When I saw who it was, I couldn't disguise the breath-taking gasp.

I came down from my high, noticing a few curious eyes though most people were into worship. I kept looking until I saw her in the fourth row, fourth seat. Lakesha stood with her arms crossed, chewing her gum and rolling her eyes at me. The mile-high weave and low bangs across her tiny head did nothing to shield heat from her eyes that pierced me like the vicious Florida sun. I had to look away.

I felt another pull on my leg and sat so I could face the imposter. *Her* child. He was standing right next to me. Lakesha must have told him to come stand by me.

The child I hadn't known existed until two days ago. The child I refused to believe was mine. Lakesha had slept with everybody. *It was only one time,* I told myself. A blunder. A poor way of handling my grief when my father died five years ago. At the time, I wasn't even sure why I was grieving the death of someone who had tormented me. I was in a state of complete confusion. Like someone who had flipped over with a capsized boat, I didn't know which way was up or down, which was the only way on earth I would have ended up lying next to that girl.

It was only because I had made something of myself that Lakesha was trying to make me the donkey to pin this on. She needed a Baby Daddy with a few zeroes in his checking account. That's what I told myself when I'd tossed her crudely written letter into the garbage.

But seeing the little boy now, I noticed a small resemblance. There was no denying this was Lakesha's kid. But was he mine?

He gave me a shy smile. I froze at the slight gap between his front teeth. He rested one little hand on my leg and curled an index finger toward his face, motioning for me to lean in.

I followed his lead.

He cupped his hands around my ear and said, "I love you, Daddy."

I croaked out some response, I don't know what. All I could think about was his voice. I knew that voice. I knew those words. The sounds of worship around me dimmed and I was transported back to a time I couldn't forget.

"I love you, Daddy."

"Shut up," Pop said. "I could never love you."

I turned and stared at Lakesha. She had told her son to say those words I had told her in confidence that night. She lifted a chin and mouthed, "What?"

I turned to face the boy again. To my horror, I found myself whispering, "I-I-man...I can't do this."

The boy's eyes filled with tears. I winced, knowing I'd crushed the heart of one so young, but I couldn't say the words he needed to hear. Lakesha's child—I couldn't call him my son—ran away from me, back to his mother. He clung to her side. Eyes narrowed into slits like shards of glass cut into me.

I grabbed my Bible. I had to get out of there. Despite all I'd gone through to get to church, I couldn't stay. I couldn't sit through a message on heroes when I knew I was that little boy's villain. All around me people praised and rejoiced, but their joy suffocated me. All I could do was run. I rushed into my car and tore out of the church parking lot where freedom awaited. I accelerated with each passing mile, welcoming the rush, tempted to leave Lovetown behind. And, I would have, except… Niya.

3

NIYA

Seeing Sean was the most exciting thing that happened to me the whole week, which was kind of sad when I thought about it. I mean, if seeing my deceased brother's best friend whom I might not see again for years was a highlight for seven days, I might as well go ahead and die now because it was going to be a long three years.

Jazzy, however, had plenty to do that week because she got her check. The state paid her eight dollars an hour to care for our grandmother 30 hours a week. It came to nearly eight hundred dollars a month after taxes, enough to keep her hair and nails done plus purchase some clothes.

I'd asked for a small share—$50 a week?—since I did occasionally put lotion on Big's feet or go to the store on her behalf.

"Really, Niya? You should be paying *me* for all the times I cook and clean for you right along with Big," my sister fussed. “Plus, I pay your phone bill on my plan. You’re a bum. I’m not gonna pay you for that.”

I couldn’t argue with her. When I had a job, I used to help out but there wasn’t any place within walking distance that was hiring. After a couple years of begging for jobs at the laundromat and even the liquor store, I’d stop trying. So, yes, I was a bum. A 27-year-old bum with nothing to look forward to except the next time I happened to be walking down the street while Sean was driving by. And then what would I do? Flag him down? And what if he stopped? Would I get in? Where would we go? What would we do?

Being in his presence had ignited something in me I hadn’t felt since junior high when I had a crush on Chandler Carraway. He was a nerdy guy with oily skin, but he was tall and muscular. Chandler always wore a hoodie, so not many girls had picked up on his body except me. I saw it once when Mr. Raymond made Chandler take off his jacket in the cafeteria when we were registering for classes. Those biceps popped out like ka-dow.

Even Jazzy had noticed. “Dang, he look good from far away.”

I downplayed the observation with, “Naaa. He’s nobody.” For the next two weeks, I’d begged my counselor to take me out of my third period class—the only seventh grade honors math class—and switch me into third period choir, the only one seventh graders could join, so I could be in class with Chandler.

“But your teachers all say you’re great at math, Niya.

Have you talked to your grandmother about going from honors to regular math?" my counselor, Ms. Martin said, squinting as she flipped through my file.

"Uh huh. She said it's okay if I go down. Everybody in my family's bad at math anyway." Though I hadn't talked to Big about dropping the class, I was telling the truth about my family being horrible math students. When I had to help Jazzy with her math homework, Big said she wasn't surprised because she'd flunked out of high school due to Algebra.

My bright-eyed, blonde-haired counselor shook her head. "If you say so." She proceeded to fill out the paper for my transfer of classes. As a 12-year-old girl, sitting in a hard, orange chair in a tiny cubicle space, I had thought that moment was the ticket to my happiness. Once Ms. Martin moved me down to regular math and signed me up for the same elective as Chandler, I would get him to like me. He would fall in love with me, we would be the "it" couple from then until twelfth grade, then I would get pregnant on our prom night, we would move into an apartment together, and we would have a baby sometime around Christmas after we graduated.

That was my dream.

After wrangling that sheet of paper from Ms. Martin's hand and spending a week in choir class with Chandler, I realized that my dream would not be coming true. Chandler didn't like black girls. I'm not even sure he liked girls at all. Furthermore, he couldn't sing.

I was too ashamed or afraid or both to ask Ms. Martin to put me back in honors, so I stayed in regular math, which meant I was ineligible for Algebra the following year and I lost the chance to take higher math classes for the rest of my high school career. Not that I wanted to sign up for that path, but I wondered what might have happened if I'd had at least one honors or AP class.

I'm not saying I would have gone to college or anything like that, but maybe if I had an honors distinction on my diploma, I could have gotten a better job so I wouldn't be sitting around hoping against hope that Jazzy might spare me twenty dollars every now and then.

As soon as the mail came Friday afternoon, she was up and out. "I'm getting braids this time, so don't wait up for me," she said, stuffing a novel into her purse. "Big's dinner is sitting in the refrigerator with foil on it. Do *not* let her put any extra salt on it. It's seasoned enough already."

"Okay," I agreed, knowing I had no intentions of enforcing Jazzy's rules. I didn't like it when she talked to me like I was her child. But it had always been this way between me and her. In fact, it was worse after Momma died. Jazzy and I were minutes apart in age, but seemingly decades apart in dominion.

Big sat in her wheelchair and I lay across the sofa for the next three hours, watching game shows. Well, I should say *she* watched television while I played games on my phone.

While I waited for the levels to load, I counted and recounted the twenty-two stripes in the peeling kitchen wallpaper on the side nearest our wobbly, wooden dining table. Despite the folded paper beneath one of its legs, the table still managed to stay annoyingly uneven. Jazmin had tried to bring a little beauty in the place with a white, plastic vase with three fake roses poking out the top. I wanted to ask her what good she thought those roses were doing when our stove looked like we'd gotten it from a church giveaway and our three overcrowded countertops were so stained, it was hard to tell what the original color had been.

Still, I had to give it to my sister. She ran through tons of bleach every month making sure that no matter how run-down our belongings were, they were at least disinfected. That rose vase included.

My connection was slow since I had used all my premium data for the month, and the internet was running on a lower speed. "Shoot," I exclaimed when I missed catching a diamond in my game because of the delay.

"Y'all gonna all need bifocals and trifocals, keeping your eyes focused on that tiny screen for hours a day," Big said under her breath.

I glanced over at her and noticed she'd gotten a new swath of gray hair. "No, we won't."

"You mark my words. You're gonna be half-blind before you hit forty."

That number, coming from her mouth to me, nearly took my breath away. *Forty?* "I thought you said everybody in our family dies young."

"Most do. But not *everybody*. I'm still here. How old you

think I am?" She poked out her lips. She gave me a glance she might have used a long time ago to flirt with a man. Even with her drooping eyelids, a forehead full of wrinkles and skin weathered because of drinking and smoking, Big still thought she was cute.

"I don't know, but…you really think I might live until forty?" I asked.

She cocked her head as though giving my question serious consideration. "Well, I mean, you don't go nowhere. You don't do nothin'. You got a pretty good chance of makin' it if you stay away from people and keep to yourself. That way you don't get into no arguments over nobody's husband. Plus people ain't sneezin' all over you. You ain't got to deal with other folks' germs. That'll keep you from cancer. I don't care what nobody say, cancer is contagious. It's in the air." She waved her plump hand in the air. "You stay home, don't pick up too much weight, you might make it to seventy-one, like me. The only thing that kept me around this long, because I know I'm big, is that I don't allow no one, nobody to stress me out."

Seventy-one.

Quickly, I did the math. *I might have 44 more years left. I'm not even at the halfway point of my life yet.*

I knew it was odd for a healthy 27-year-old to think about how many years she had left to live. But after losing my mother, my father, and my brother along with countless others in my family far too soon, death seemed almost imminent…until that very moment.

I'd only half-played the games on my phone afterward. And I'd even let Big put extra salt on her chicken. I figured if she'd made it to the ripe old age of 21, she should be able to eat whatever she wanted.

I took Big to her room, took my own shower, and got into bed.

Sleep, however, didn't come to me. *What will I look like when I'm seventy-one? Big will be dead by then. Where will Jazzy and I live? What's Jazzy going to do for work then? Will I need to get a job, too?*

Then, I did the math on the idea of me getting a job. If I got a job making eight dollars an hour and Jazzy had a job making eight dollars an hour, we'd have almost two thousand dollars a month. We could afford to stay anywhere we wanted. We might even get a car together. And driver's licenses. And insurance.

For as different as Jazzy and I had always been, I still thought of my life as "our" life. I couldn't imagine not being with her.

Jazzy snuck in the house a little after ten. I turned on the lamp on the nightstand between our beds so I could see her hair.

She entered our room with a smile on her face and braids down to her behind. "You like?"

"Yeah," I said, admiring how the tiny braids flowed over her shoulder as she bent to unsnap her sandals. "Who did it?"

"Shayna."

"How much did she charge?" I inquired.

"Eighty-five, but I had to buy my own hair. Five bags."

"Oh," I nearly growled, adding the figures and realizing the style had cost anywhere from $120-$150.

"Big ate?" Jazzy asked.

"Yes."

Before she could ask about the salt, I changed the subject. "Did I tell you I saw Sean the other day?"

"Yeah. You told me."

"Oh. Okay. Just wanted to make sure."

"And I saw that *gleam* in your eye when you told me about him," she teased.

"I did *not* have a gleam." I shook my head. Though I didn't appreciate her teasing me, I reveled in the fact that Jazzy and I were having one of our rare closed-door, sister-to-sister moments.

"Whatever. Don't get your hopes up. Lakesha Billings is trying to either get with him or get back at him," Jazzy said. She carefully slid her sling purse over her head and under the mass of what had to be 22-inch braids. She set the purse back in its place on the closet doorknob.

I sat up. "Wait—what? Lakesha Billings? Sean was with *her*?"

"He's not *with* her. At least not now. But he might have been with her in the past. Shayna said Lakesha was there earlier, before I got there, getting an updo. I guess Shayna knows you don't like Lakesha so she assumed I don't like her either, that's why she waited to text me and tell me exactly when to come, so I wouldn't run into Lakesha."

"Shayna assumed right. Right?" I cocked my head. Even though Jazzy and I were two very different people, she was still my sister. My twin. She was supposed to like who I liked, despise who I despised.

"Yes. I don't like Lakesha because you don't like her, if that makes you happy." Jazzy wagged her head. "But I mean, personally, I don't have anything against her." She continued undressing down to her underclothes.

I let my head slip back onto the pillow, though I was still listening.

"Anyway, Shayna said Lakesha told her that Sean ran out of church when she showed him his son."

"Is it his kid?" I asked as though Jazzy should know the answer.

"Shayna said the boy looks like Sean. She also said the boy is bad. Like really, really bad. Jumping on her furniture. Wouldn't stop playing with her stuff even after his mom told him to stop. He even tried to hit her puppy."

My chest deflated. Sean and Lakesha? Sean had a son *and* the kid was bad?

Jazzy changed into her nightgown as she continued the story. "Shayna said Lakesha was saying Sean is stable and she wants to move in with him so they can be a family. He lives in those new apartments about a mile past Mr. Henderson's store. Lakesha trailed him and found out where he lives."

My eyes widened. "She's a stalker."

Niya shrugged. "No, not if Sean *is* her baby daddy. He's

not supposed to be living all high and mighty while she's struggling to raise his kid all by herself."

"Okay, but he ran out of church, so maybe he is *not* the father," I said in my Maury Povich voice.

Jazzy hung up her pants in the closet and sighed. "Niya. Really? Do you think it's a good idea to try to get with Jhavon's best friend? Sean is like a brother to us. He's like Jhavon number two. It might be too hard to separate your feelings for him from your feelings for our brother."

My sister created a part down the middle of her head, separating the braids into two sections. Then she braided them into two giant ropes, putting rubber bands at the bottom.

I laid back flat on the bed. "I never said I liked Sean. I only said I *saw* him."

"Niya. We're twins. Did you forget? I know what you're feeling." She wrapped a silk scarf around her hairline.

I couldn't deny this annoying truth.

"Give it up." She clicked off the lamp.

Her bed creaked as she dove beneath the covers.

In the darkness, I could still see the outline of her body. She was turned onto one side, which meant she was nowhere near zzzzs. I still had time to probe her brain.

"You ever think about what we'll be like when we're Big's age? When we're seventy-one?"

"No. We might not make it to seventy-one. Momma, Daddy, and Jhavon didn't. People die every day."

"But what if we *do* survive?" I pressed.

"Then we'd be old. Nobody wants to be old. That's depressing."

I wondered aloud, "You think we'll still live in this house? In this room?"

"No. I'll move to Big's room," she stated. "You can stay here in this room."

The words, "I don't want to stay in this room forever," came rushing out from somewhere inside me.

"Well, you're not getting Big's room. It's mine. I just called it. Night."

In that split second of time, I knew there was no way I was going to spend the next 44 years of my life in that same bed, that same room, sleeping against that same dingy wall.

Something had to change.

4

SEAN

"You should have never bought the ticket and rode that train. She's travelled around the block enough times to circle the world. *Twice,"* Travis said.

"I agree," Mike replied. "Lakesha hasn't just been around the block. She's the whole building. Everybody done rode up and down that elevator a few times."

I winced. I guess I deserved them ragging on me. They loved the ladies but neither had gone there with Lakesha, and it wasn't because she hadn't tried.

Standing outside on the patio by the huge outdoor grill I'd bought on sale at Lowe's, I let the conversation carry on behind me once I'd unloaded my news about Lakesha and what happened at church. I found comfort in the mundane task of cleaning the steaks and seasoning them with my special marinade while Travis and Mike hashed out the latest drama of my life.

Travis chuckled. "Dang, Mike. That's cold. You know you wrong to talk about Sean's baby mama like that."

I clenched my jaw and turned, facing the men sitting at the glass table. "I don't know if he's mine for sure."

"You don't know if he *isn't* yours either," Travis shot back.

"Back off," Mike said. "Ain't nothing funny about having a child. A son."

"No, but Sean's *face* is funny," Travis said, cracking up.

"You joke too much," I said to Travis. "And you're the one with the funny face. The *mystery* face. What is it, anyway? Black? White? Hispanic?"

Travis, used to questions and jokes about his multi-ethnic background, shook his head while pointing to himself. "Don't hate. Appreciate this melting pot right here."

"Anyway," I continued. "This is a disruption in my life. My plans…" I couldn't find the words so I stomped inside to get the bag of sweet potatoes, corn, and foil paper. When I returned, I dumped them on the table and instructed Travis, "Do something useful besides running your mouth. Wrap the corn and potatoes. Do y'all do that in your culture?"

"Which one?" Travis laughed, taking up the task.

"Is it really the end of the world to claim a fatherless child?" Mike asked, picking up a potato to assist.

I tensed. Mike had been adopted by his grandparents

after he was abandoned by his mother, who was addicted to meth.

"This is isn't the same thing," I tried to explain, mindful of Mike's past. "This is different. Your grand—I mean parents—are good people. I'm… I'm me."

"And let's not forget this child might not be Sean's," Travis said. "Why should he claim another man's child?"

"Jesus did." Mike gave me a pointed look as if to say I should know this.

I wiped my brow. "Jesus is God so you can't compare me to Him."

Mike ripped off a splice of foil from the roll and picked up an ear of corn. "Don't you church folk have a saying…" He squinted. "You're the only God people see or something like that."

"Well, like the man said, he's nowhere near close to God," Travis said.

I knew he was only trying to help my cause, but Travis' words made me feel hollow. Shallow. I couldn't look Mike in the eyes or give him the good Christian answer. I wanted to rage and holler, not talk about the goodness of Jesus and all He had done for me.

"I don't expect you to be on God's level but your attitude on this fatherhood thing is...surprising." Mike returned to his task.

My shoulders drooped at the disappointment in Mike's voice. I knew I was failing both him and God, but I couldn't pretend. The thought of being that child's father shook my very core. I made my way to the grill and placed the mesquite wood chips on top of the coals and searched for the butane lighter. Within seconds, a huge flame kindled. I stepped away from the searing heat, mesmerized by the flames licking at the mesquite chips.

That's how I felt. Like that chip. And Lakesha was the fire that was about to burn out my very existence.

Travis came and stood next to me. He put a hand on my shoulder. "Don't look so dejected. Once the shock wears off, you'll know what to do. It will all work out."

I shrugged, thinking I might be in this comatose state for a while. But I strove to express the magnitude of what I felt. "I don't get it. I was always so careful. How am I ending up just like my old man—a terrible father? I mean, I'm not abusive or anything, but there's a lot of different ways to be a horrible parent, starting with being absent."

"Life happens," Mike said. He brought over the foil-wrapped vegetables and placed them on the tray next to the grill.

Once the embers settled and the coal began to smoke, I put the steaks on.

Travis looked at his watch and mumbled something under his breath.

"What's with you, man? This is the third time you're looking at your watch," I asked.

Travis gave a sheepish grin. "You saw that? I was looking out for a text from Jazmin. I was asking if she wanted to do something later for her birthday."

"And you expected her to answer?" Mike laughed. "You know Jazmin is into Big and her books. She has no room for anyone else."

Birthday? I felt my eyes go wide. How could I have forgotten Niya's birthday? The entire time we were together this morning, she must have wondered why I didn't say anything. "Birthday?" I said aloud.

"Yeah," Travis said. "I thought that's why you went to see your girl, Niya, this morning."

I shook my head. "No… I…"

"See that's why you need to be on Instagram and Snapchat like the rest of the normal world. You would never miss another birthday."

"I don't like people in my business like that," I said.

"Wait. What do you mean, his girl?" Mike asked, butting in. "Is there something going on I need to know about?"

I ignored Mike's question. I wasn't ready to have a conversation with him about my emerging feelings for Niya, especially after his innuendos this morning. I had admitted my feelings to Travis when I'd called to ask him to collect my keys, air out my apartment and turn on the AC since I'd signed my lease remotely.

"So, I guess nobody's going to answer my question?" Mike asked again, interrupting my thoughts. He looked between us before flailing his hands. "Aight. Cool. I see how it is."

"Ain't my story to tell," Travis said, swatting at a fly. He jutted his chin my way. "Let me text you Niya's number."

"Cool. Thanks," I said. I dug into my jeans pocket, took out my phone, and sent Niya a birthday text. I kept my phone in my hand to wait for her response.

Travis decided to fill the sudden quiet with a question. "What I want to know is, how you plan on explaining your baby mom—ugh—I mean, Lakesha to Niya. Those two can't stand each other. They've been at each other's throats since high school. Their rivalry is of epic proportions."

Mike challenged me with a knowing look.

I shrugged. I knew I had to say something then. "This is all brand new. We'll talk."

He gave me a thumbs up, signaling he could wait. Then he added, "They can't be in the same room without a cat fight." He watched me as he spoke to ascertain my reaction.

I kept my expression neutral and returned to the grill to turn the steaks and put on the corn and potatoes.

"It's roasting hot out here," Travis said. "I'm going inside to get some of that fresh-squeezed lemonade you pride yourself on making."

"Bring me a glass," Mike said, coming over to me. He sniffed. "That smells good. You got my mouth watering."

I looked at my watch. "It'll probably be about twenty minutes or so and we can dig in." I gestured toward the kitchen. "Why don't you get the salad together? Make yourself useful."

Mike looked like he wanted to say something but it appeared his stomach won out. He strolled into the house, leaving me free to think about the dilemma of these two women. One I wanted in my life and the other seemed to be inserting her way into my path without invitation. Just my luck they were arch enemies.

The feud had started somewhere in middle school when they both tried out for the cheer and dance squad. Lakesha had made captain. I had to give it to her. When I watched her at the football games, I knew that girl had some serious moves.

According to rumor, the dance coach found out about Lakesha's escapade with a boy in a school restroom and demoted her from captain because she was setting a bad example for the team. Niya was named captain, by no request of her own, but that title put her at odds with Lakesha. Then there was a bunch of mess with Lakesha and her minions trying to sabotage Niya's leadership, Jazzy—who wasn't even on the team—making threats to anybody who messed with her sister, and Niya doing her best to keep the team from breaking into two cliques. Finally, the coach pried the truth out of Niya, which resulted in Lakesha getting kicked off the squad permanently. Since then, those two had bad blood. So bad even the counselors at the school knew not to schedule them for the same classes.

The truth was, putting aside all that cheer and dance drama, Niya outshined Lakesha on so many levels. For one thing, Niya kept her pearl inside her clam. Lakesha constantly had hers on display. Which is why I knew it was my guilt and grief that led me to get under the covers with Lakesha, or rather, in the back seat of my father's rickety old

Jeep. I shook my head. I didn't know how I would tell Niya that I'd not only slept with Lakesha but had a child with her as well.

Well, allegedly. *Nothing had been proven yet.*

I sighed. This wasn't how I imagined my first weeks back in Lovetown would go. After being honorably discharged, I had begun using the communications degree I earned to connect people with jobs as a corporate recruiter. I helped other young people land their dream jobs. A little bit of mentoring came with the job, but that wouldn't start until September. In the meantime, my only plans were to enjoy my new place, hang with my friends, and explore a relationship with Niya.

Never did I once imagine there would be a child waiting to look at me with soulful brown eyes and say, "I love you, Daddy."

My cell pinged.

I smiled. It was Niya.

Thank you, she said with a happy face emoji. My insides relaxed when she didn't come at me asking how I had gotten her number.

I quickly texted back. *Want to go to Painting with Friends tonight?* Then I felt foolish. I should've called her like the grown man I am. Not ask her out on a potential first date using text.

Can't today. Another time? She texted back.

I wasn't about to be discouraged. *How about this Thursday?*

See you then.

Yes! Niya had agreed to a date. I imagined her beautiful face lit up, smiling at my text.

After all these years, I was finally going on my first date with Niya. The first of many if I had my way.

5

NIYA

I still had Sean's text saved in my phone. I couldn't delete it because...I don't know...it was important. What if he never asked me to go out with him again after tonight? The saved text would be a memento. Proof that one day, a long time ago, somebody wanted to go somewhere with me.

True, guys at school had asked me out before but most of them just wanted one thing. I had no intentions of letting my first time happen with some guy who didn't even know my last name or who couldn't tell me apart from my sister.

Jazzy had felt the same way. But once we turned twenty, Jazzy crossed over with a dude named Fegan Parkerson. She had met him at the beauty supply store. He was new in town and claimed to be getting oil sheen for his "mother." True to our generation, Fegan and Jazzy didn't go out on any actual dates. They texted and met up to hook up. Three months after their trysts started, Jazzy learned his "mother" was his wife. Jazzy was so hurt by the incident that, after she slashed his tires, she vowed never to be so gullible again. She still had boyfriends here and there, but she didn't allow herself to trust any man. Her heroes were found in the pages of her romance novels, not in real life.

The situation with Fegan put a double-edge to her already sharp demeanor. The only two things she trusted besides me were books and Big.

Most people in Lovetown probably thought me and Jazzy were stuck-up because we didn't get around with men much. Or, in my case, at all. The ones who wanted more than a quick fix with me wanted too much too fast. I've heard everything from "Let's get our names tattooed on each other" to "You're beautiful. Will you be my first baby momma?"

I knew things with Sean would be different if for no other reason than I knew he wasn't interested in "one thing" and he was saved. He had two things going for him.

But was I confusing my feelings for him with memories of Jhavon, like Jazzy said? And what if things didn't work out between us? Would that mean our connection would be severed? I mean, he and I weren't "close" in the traditional sense. It was kind of a see-you-when-I-see-you situation, but I think that was because he'd been gone so long and because there was a lot of pain between us since Jhavon died.

And what if he'd also asked Lakesha to spend time with him? Did he want to be with her and her son?

Though the what-ifs plagued me, I still found myself

brushing my natural hair into an updo at 6:00, anticipating Sean's 6:30 arrival and our 7:00 painting class.

"You look cute," Jazzy complimented me. "You should wear my gold heels. That'll go real good with that white blouse and jeans."

"Wait. Should I be wearing a white blouse? We're painting, remember?"

"I'm sure they'll give you something to cover up. Let's fix the shoe situation." She tossed her current novel onto the bed, retrieved said shoes from her side of the closet, and presented them to me as I examined myself in the mirror one last time.

I wrinkled my nose. "I can't wear those. The heel's way too high. I'd step on a crack and break my *own* back."

Jazzy thrust the shoes into my stomach. "No, you won't. Just walk slow. And if you stumble, Sean will catch you."

I shoved the shoes back toward her. "But—"

"Niya, stop. You're not a kid. And this date with Sean is serious. It's corny, but it's serious. He likes you, you like him. You gotta pay attention to what's happening tonight so you can figure out your real feelings."

I sighed, taking in the uneasy expression on my face. "You're right. I am a grown woman. And this time with Sean tonight is important." I took the shoes from my sister and put them on my feet. As soon as I did, they rubbed my pinky toe the wrong way.

"Ow," I yelped. "These shoes are torture."

"It's the price of beauty. Now. Do you have protection?" she asked.

I rolled my eyes. "What? No, what? Like a knife or something?"

"Really? Niya. No. I'm talking about protection from getting pregnant."

This suggestion seemed just as absurd as me carrying around a knife. "Are you kidding me?"

Jazzy looked me in the eyes and shook her head. "Niya, I know this is all brand new to you. But Sean is a man. A sexy man, at that. And you're cute 'cause you look a lot like me." She winked and gave a smirk. "He's got his own place, too."

"Are you serious? I don't think Sean would try anything. Or did you forget he's saved?" I tried to cancel her concerns.

"Please. This is a tale as old as time. Boy meets girl. They're attracted. Anything can happen. We've both made it this far without having any kids. Don't add to the problems I already have taking care of us and Big."

She'd done it again. Come for me like she was my parent, my guardian, my lifeline. I put a hand on my hip. "If I *did* get pregnant by somebody, you wouldn't have to worry about raising the baby. That would be my responsibility."

"Just don't let it happen. Enjoy your little painting date with Sean. I wanna know if he's gonna say anything about his baby momma, so I'll wait up to listen to the whole story when you get back. No secrets. Okay?"

I rolled my eyes but still agreed.

When Sean arrived, he greeted Big. They shared a hug

and reminisced about Jhavon. "You remember when I spanked both of y'all for painting my dog?" she asked.

"I'll never forget it," he said, showing his pearly whites.

Then they both started laughing.

Big's tiny house was so small. We could hear conversations from all directions.

Per Jazzy's instructions, I waited five minutes before presenting myself.

It worked. Big had half-talked off Sean's ear, so my entrance was a refreshing interruption, according to the look on his face. His eyes shot up, his mouth dropped, and his gaze swept my entire body from top to bottom.

"You look great," he complimented me as he rose from Big's tattered love seat.

"Thank you."

From under my lashes, I studied Sean's skin that was a sea of caramel, contrasted with deep, dark eyebrows and lush brown lips. I wet my lips with the tip of my tongue. The few times I had seen him around town, his body moved like a superhero, guided in its sway by his muscular shoulders. I could feel my pulse beating in my ear.

Jazzy was right. *Anything could happen.*

Sean drove us to Red Valley, which was filled with fast food restaurants and clothing stores I had never even heard of. When I shared my observation with Sean, he explained how many of the traditional fast-food chains had been bought out by up-and-coming companies who wanted to prepare healthier choices. Some of them had even replaced beef with tofu.

"But everybody ain't gonna give up meat," I said.

Sean shrugged. "Some will."

Is he crazy? His nonchalant response gave me pause. Why was he saying those things? Everybody I knew ate meat three times a day. "Have you gone without meat?"

"Yeah. Plenty of times. I've gone whole days without eating anything," he added.

I envisioned Sean starving, laying out on the ground, skinny, looking pitiful with a tin can in hand utilized as a collection plate because "no food" meant "no money" in my world.

"Are you serious? In my experience, the only reason a person didn't eat meat was because they were homeless, jobless, didn't have family, or were unconscious or something."

He chuckled. "I've broadened my horizons. To me, it's just food. There's plenty more where that came from."

His way of thinking about food was so foreign to me, I began to wonder if going off and seeing the world had made Sean out of touch with reality. Sean and Jhavon had been so much alike, but there was no way Jhavon would have said anything so crazy like not eating meat or food every day.

Sean had changed. I needed to get that in my head. I rubbed my chin, maybe change was good. This might help me see him as Sean, not just Jhavon's best friend who used to eat up all the bologna in the kitchen when he came over.

We arrived at a small shopping center, and Sean parked the roaring Mustang far from the stores despite the empty spots nearer.

"Why'd you park so far away?"

He slid a glance my way. "Gotta try to protect my paint job. Don't want no door dings from people parked too close."

Really? If having a car was this much trouble, I didn't want one, given how far we had to walk to the front. And in these heels, too.

My face must have told on me.

"You okay? I mean, I can drop you off at the front." He put his hand on the key, preparing to switch on the ignition if I said so.

"No. I'm fine." I unbuckled my seatbelt. Then I smiled and gave myself permission to speak my mind. "But I might as well have walked here as far as we are from the entrance."

He busted out laughing. "Oh, you got jokes, huh?"

I laughed, too, and suddenly realized the best part of Sean was still there. Good humored. Easy.

Our hands dangled close as we walked toward the painting studio. I hoped he would take my hand into his, but he didn't. Maybe he was trying to be respectful. Maybe I was just overthinking everything.

Calm down, Niya. It's only Sean.

The venue was bright and colorful, as I would expect such a place to be. Walls were filled with canvas paintings of intricate, difficult-to-paint scenes—a woman with a large hat, a dandelion with leaves that had depth, an ocean-side sunset with various hues of purple and blue. How on earth was I supposed to create something as beautiful as these paintings?

"Hi!" A chipper, red-haired young woman wearing a black smock with the company's logo greeted us. "You here for the seven o'clock class?"

"Yes. Sean and Niya," he said.

A smile escaped. I liked the way our names sounded together.

The attendant searched her computer screen, clicked her mouse a few times. "Gotcha checked in. You can go on into Studio B. Grab a smock and a seat. Your instructor's already inside."

I followed Sean's lead, feeling the fear of failure rise up within me.

Sean and I made more small talk as the instructor began the class. First, there was talk about safety and handling materials. Sean didn't seem to be paying attention, but I sure was. I could barely draw stick figures. It occurred to me that perhaps I could stand behind Sean and watch the process over his broad shoulders, but I knew that wasn't going to happen after I saw the sign telling me he'd paid $35 apiece for our tickets. For $35, I was gonna have a brush in my hand and some paint on my own canvas.

"Tonight, we're painting Owl on a Branch."

I gave Sean a what-in-the-world glare.

He winked at me and whispered, "Keep an open mind. Owls are a symbol for wisdom."

The wink, of course, disarmed me. Melted me might have been a better description of what happened to my insides under his gaze.

A few minutes later, with a smock tied over my clothing and the heels tossed under my table, I made my first stroke on the blank, white canvas. It seemed odd to mess it up with the light blue paint I'd mixed. Even as I began to fill the sky area, I wondered if I had mixed enough to cover all the area I'd need. What if I ran out and the shade wasn't a perfect match?

My mind screamed that I should have left it blank so I wouldn't mess up.

As if on cue, the instructor said, "Don't worry about messing up your painting. This is art. It's not perfect. Neither is life. It's okay."

I relaxed my shoulders and let out a deep breath.

"You okay?" Sean asked. "You seem kind of stressed."

I spoke with the same speed as the slow, methodical gliding of the paint brush, fearing I might lose control of the brush if I spoke too fast. "I'm not good at painting. This is hard."

"Yeah." He shrugged. "But I love a good challenge. Reminds me of school."

His comment snapped me back to my real self. I scoffed. "School wasn't hard. It was just boring."

"I can see why you're saying that. You were always a

genius. Jhavon said so. He said you always got good grades though you barely even tried."

A smile slid across my face. My brother had told me that, too.

"He always thought you'd go to college," Sean added.

That I didn't know. I plopped my paintbrush into the cup of rinsing water. "When did he say that?"

"All the time," Sean said, sticking his tongue between his teeth, while he focused on the branch for his owl. I watched him work until he put the brush down to tap me on the nose. "He said it wouldn't surprise him if you grew up to be a doctor or a teacher."

I warned my heart to stop accelerating at his playful touch and concentrated on his words. I uttered an eloquent, "Huh," before dipping my brush in solid brown to start my own branch. Sean returned to his painting while I mulled over his words.

My brother had told me countless times that I was smart. People told me that all the time. But none of that had mattered after I finished high school. Employers don't know how smart you are when they're reading your application online. The few times I had worked seasonal jobs, nobody had asked me to stay past Christmas or summer, so obviously I wasn't like "real-world" smart.

Big wasn't a particular fan of college. She said the worst thing in the world was an "educated fool" and people who forgot where they came from. I never wanted to be either and college probably would have qualified me for both.

"You ever thought about going to college?" Sean asked, nudging me on the shoulder.

There he goes touching me again. "No." I said the word with enough edge to let him know I didn't want to talk about it, but Sean was persistent.

"So...what did you want to be in your life?"

I rubbed my hand on my thigh and twisted my lips to the side. This time I allowed myself to dream. "Doctor sounded good, but we all know that ain't gonna happen."

"Why not?"

"Because I didn't go to college," I said with a 'duh' in my tone.

"What's stopping you now?" he asked.

"I'm twenty-seven," I reminded him. "Way too old for all that now."

"There's no age limit on when you can go to college," he said.

I furrowed my brows. This was new information for me. I'd never heard of a twenty-seven year old person going to college for the first time. When I saw students on TV at college football games, they all looked like they'd just finished high school a week earlier. Nineteen, twenty-one years old at the most. Schools wouldn't let a 10-year old sit in kindergarten so why would they allow me to attend college at age 27?

I asked the question in a roundabout way. "What would I look like sitting in a classroom with 18-year-olds?"

"I think you'd look smart. Wise. And pretty."

His words made my insides shiver all the way down to my toes. *Smart. Wise. And pretty.*

The instructor interrupted my thoughts. "Let the picture speak to you," she said. Then she turned on classical music. I stopped looking at Sean's work and the work of my classmates and did my own thing. My brain took me from Sean and even from the room as I decided my owl would not be black. He would be purple because purple was my favorite color. And I made his eyes gold because that particular paint was metallic. I wanted his eyes to shine.

Smart. Wise. And pretty.

I stuck my tongue between my teeth. If I were smart, wise, and pretty, then painting this picture was going to be my first glimpse into that prophecy.

I tuned into the instructor's guidance, watching everything from the colors she chose to the way she flicked her brush as she ended the branch strokes. All I had to do was do what she did. And when I messed up, I followed her advice.

"Just keep going. Let it dry for a little bit, use white if you need to cover something, or you can make something new out of the mistake—another branch, another feather. Those imperfections are what make it *yours*."

When I raised my hand for help, she came over and asked permission to show me how to put the reflection in one of the owl's eyes. I tried the trick on the other eye, and it worked. "You got this," she encouraged me.

Sean smiled and it took everything in me not to dive into him with a big kiss.

He took me straight home after the class and set my painting on the front porch so it could continue to dry in the hot night air.

"Thanks again for inviting me to the class. I really enjoyed myself."

"It was my pleasure. Your painting turned out good," he complimented me.

My chest puffed. "Thanks. Yours was aiiight."

He held a fist up to his mouth. "Oh, you wanna get fly about it now?"

We laughed.

"Seriously, though, think about college. You can apply and probably be able to start next semester," he said.

I gave a little nod. "I'll think about it."

"You should. You've got what it takes to be whatever you want to be. Just like you learned to paint listening to that lady and following directions, you can do the same thing with school. Just listen, practice, learn from your mistakes. That's all anyone who's ever done anything with their lives did. No magic to it."

"Stop." I waved him off. "That's what they tell us when we're five. But if it's true, why is everybody so miserable?"

"Everybody's not miserable. Just the people who want to be."

Sean hugged me, but it felt like a 'you're-my-friend's-little-sister' hug. My mouth yearned to feel those full lips against mine, but maybe we weren't ready for all that yet.

"Night, Niya," he whispered, his baritone sounding even lower than normal.

"Good night, Sean."

I went inside and breezed past Jazzy, who was waiting just inside the door.

"No kiss?" she fussed.

"No. It wasn't like that," I said, throwing the shoes off my feet. I couldn't wait to get in bed and massage my hurting toes. I walked toward our room, but Jazzy stopped me with a firm grip on my shoulder.

"Well...what was it like?" she asked.

"We just had a good time together at the painting place." I shrugged.

She placed a hand on her hip. "What did he say about Lakesha?"

"Nothing. Nothing at all."

Jazzy rolled her eyes. "He sorry and you *almost* as sorry as him. How come you didn't ask Sean about his supposed-to-be son and his baby momma?"

I offered her my upturned palms. "I don't know. I mean, I was painting. And having a good time. I didn't want to bring it up."

"Well, you needed to bring it up. You need to know if you need to watch your back with that girl and if he's gonna be a deadbeat dad. That's important. Big taught us that, remember?"

"Yeah. I do." My sister was right. I couldn't be with Sean if he wasn't doing right by his kid. My father was far from perfect, but one thing Jazzy and I had that most of our friends didn't, was a dad. He was one good memory from my childhood that I held dearly.

"Where's Big?" I changed the subject.

"In bed. She tried to wait up for you."

I asked, "You think she's sleep?"

"I don't know."

I took six steps down the hallway and quietly twisted the doorknob.

"Come on in," Big grunted.

I stepped inside her room. "I wanted to say good night is all."

"Mmm hmm. How'd it go?" she asked.

"It was fine. Sean is nice."

"I figured as much."

I scrunched my nose. Big didn't sound like herself. Her voice sounded kind of weak to me. I cocked my head, but Big started rambling and put my mind at ease.

"Yeah. He's always been a good boy despite his ig-nut daddy, God rest his...well, I don't know if that man's soul is restin' or not, come to think of it. But Sean, he's all right in my book."

I nodded, though I doubted she could see me in the darkness.

I played with my belt buckle for a moment, then stepped closer to her bed. "Big, what do you think about me going to college?"

"College ain't for everybody," she said. "And it ain't

cheap, either. That's why most folks don't go. You got to come from money to go to college, elsewise can't nobody afford it."

The college-bubble in my chest burst and flattened. Big was right. There was no way I could pay for college. No way in heaven or on earth. "Night, Big."

"Mmm hmm."

I stepped out of the room, softly closing the door behind me. I stood frozen, my mind running numbers in my head. Forty hours a week, $7.50 an hour. Eight if I was lucky. *How much would I need?* I could get two jobs. But how would I have time to go to class or study? Maybe I could go to school part-time.

I opened Big's door again and asked, "How much does college cost anyway?" When Big didn't answer, I repeated the question. "How much, Big?"

No answer again. *There's no way she fell asleep that fast.*

I approached her bed, turning on the night light.

Her eyes were open but her gaze was fixed upward. "Big." I shook her. No response. "Big. Big!"

6

NIYA

"Jazzy," I screamed.

My loud screech brought her rushing into Big's room.

"Something's happening to Big," I huffed. As though I hadn't shaken Big's body enough, Jazzy joined me in the effort. We screamed "Big" in unison, chanting, "Big? Big? Wake up."

Suddenly, Jazzy stopped. "Call 9-1-1," she ordered, her chest heaving.

I dashed into my room and dialed the number.

"Nine-one-one. Where is your emergency?" the voice asked while my heart thundered.

My lips trembled as I rattled off our address and informed the operator that my grandmother was not moving.

"Is she breathing?"

I shook my head, though she couldn't see. I wiped a sweaty hand on the front of my jeans. "Um...I don't know."

"Go get a hand mirror and put it under her nose to see if it fogs up," the woman instructed me.

With pure adrenaline pumping through my veins, I couldn't think. *Where's a mirror?*

Jazzy burst into our bedroom. "Are they coming?"

"I need a mirror," I cried out.

"A mirror for what?" she yelled back at me, tears filling her eyes.

"To check for breathing." I handed the phone to Jazzy, then skittered back to Big's room. I opened the top drawer of her dresser with such force that it slid out of place. The contents spilled on the carpeted floor. I fell to my knees and searched for Big's old compact in a pile of knick-knacks.

"Where is it? Where is it? Where is it?" My hands shook and sweat ran down my face and arms. Tears began to blur my vision. "Big, where is it?" I bellowed, knowing she couldn't answer.

After what felt like hours instead of seconds, I located an age-old container of what Big called "ruige" and snapped it open to reveal a mirror. I lifted my hands in triumph. "Finally." *Thank you, God.*

But as soon as I realized what I was about to do—determine if my grandmother was still alive—my entire body froze.

Jazzy sprinted to my side. "Give me that." She grabbed the makeup from my hand, jumped onto the bed, and held it under Big's nose with one hand while holding onto my phone with the other.

I couldn't watch. But I had to. My feet backed me into a corner as I watched my sister spring into action.

"Yes, she's breathing," I heard Jazzy say to the operator.

Breathe. Take deep breaths, I told myself as my body shivered.

I registered Jazzy's words. "Okay. I can feel her pulse. Barely," she said.

This can't be happening.

The walls seemed to close in around me as the room turned darker. I heard sirens in the distance that grew stronger, closer until the sounds were so loud, I closed my eyes and held my head. Then there was pounding...Wait. *Was that the door?*

"Don't just stand there, Niya. Go let them in," Jazzy commanded, hovering over Big.

I eased off the wall and raced to open the door.

The next few minutes were a blur. The paramedics ripping down the hallway. Asking Jazzy questions. Jazzy asking me questions I couldn't answer. "I was just...just talking to her. Then I stepped out of the room for a second. I came back in, and she wasn't talking anymore."

Jazzy gave them her medications. They strapped Big to a gurney and whizzed her past me.

"Who's riding with us?" they asked.

"I am," Jazzy answered without question. "Call the fam," she shot at me before jumping inside.

And just like that, my grandmother and my twin sister were gone to the hospital, leaving me alone in Big's house to wonder what in the world had just happened. I wiped my forehead. Would I ever see Big again? And why couldn't I think under pressure like Jazzy?

But I couldn't sit around waiting for answers. I had to get to the hospital and the only person I knew with a car who would still be up was Sean.

7

SEAN

"I'd like to get to the hospital alive," Niya hollered once she'd finished calling her family.

I cut around the curve at least 30 miles above the recommended limit before reassuring her. "Relax, I know what I'm doing."

Niya's eyes were wide and filled with fear. "Keep your eyes on the road."

"I know these roads like the back of my hands. I was one of the best drivers in combat drills," I said, though I did ease off the gas.

She folded her arms and pouted. "All it takes is one small slip and…"

I swallowed to keep from arguing and kept my eyes on the road. I had just pulled into my parking garage when I received Niya's frantic call. If Niya thought I was speeding now, she wouldn't have survived my dash back to her house.

My cell pinged with a message. I glanced down for a moment.

"Are you crazy," Niya screamed, snatching the phone from its place on my thigh. "Do not read text messages as you drive."

Though we were in a serious situation, trying to reach the hospital in record time, a part of me was amused by her anxiety. "Sorry." I feigned an apology. I kept my eyes forward to hide my thoughts. Niya was a scaredy-cat. I would enjoy bringing a sense of security into her life. I could be her hero.

Once we were at a stoplight, I reached for the phone. Niya rolled her eyes but didn't complain. I pulled up the message, angling the phone so Niya could see my screen if she wanted. After all, I had nothing to hide. I stifled a groan when I saw Lakesha's text.

Just so you know, your son cries for you at night.

I threw the phone in the center console and pressed the gas.

Niya and I finished the ride in silence but I could see her chewing on her bottom lip, like she was deep in thought. I prayed that her mind was consumed with thoughts of Big and not of Lakesha.

My gut told me she was waiting for me to explain that text message, but I wasn't volunteering information. The silence nagged at me, begging me to open my mouth, tackle the proverbial elephant in the car, but I kept my mouth clamped shut. What was I going to say? Lakesha was tripping over a kid that wasn't mine. I rubbed my brow. Besides, there was a possibility Niya hadn't seen the text. Highly unlikely, but a man could hope.

I pulled up to the hospital curb by the emergency room's double-doors. Niya mumbled a quick, "I'm going in," before opening the door. She scurried through the automatic doors without a backward glance. Yep. She had read the text. Emitting another huge sigh, I went to look for parking.

Once I claimed a spot, I recovered the phone from its resting place and viewed the message from Lakesha again. Anger pumped through my veins. What did she expect me to do—drop everything and rush over there to do what? Hug the boy and wipe his tears when I didn't even know if he was my child? My chest heaved. And even if he were my son, I wouldn't be trying to pacify that boy. I'd teach him to man up. Stop being a punk. Thump him in the chest and tell him to suck it up. *Like my father used to...*

My body released the anger like air going out of a balloon. I refused to allow myself to finish the thought. I used to hate it when my father did that to me. I lowered my head as a memory surfaced.

It was the week after my mother ran off, leaving me at eight years old to deal with an angry man. I was in second grade and outside riding my bike with friends when I made a sharp turn, fell into a ditch, and cut my knee real bad. Travis and Jhavon helped me get home. My knee was bleeding profusely and the tears flowed from not only the pain but the sight of it all.

The first thing my dad said was, "Shut up and stop crying

like a girl." He didn't ask how it happened or if I had any other injuries. He took me to the hospital. As we sat waiting to be seen, I remember him sitting there with his arms folded across his chest. Annoyed. I was trying with everything in me not to cry or make a sound. I couldn't help my yelp when the doctor injected anesthetic. Thankfully, that was the last bit of pain at the hospital.

The stitches were removed after a week or so, but my dad took my bike for what seemed like months. He said if I didn't have enough sense not to ride into a ditch, I didn't need a bike. I made the mistake of trying to tell him it was an accident.

The backhand came quicker than I could move. My cheek stung well into the night when I went to bed.

This was all I knew of fathers. Tough love, Pop called it. I used to wonder if there was such a thing as "soft" love, or just "regular" love.

Well. Anyway. My thought pattern proved I was in no position to raise a kid. Too messed up in the head, I admitted to myself. Maybe if I had a wife or something, she'd bring in the "soft" but there was no way it could come from me. Not now. Not until God finished some stuff in me because my first instincts were a replay of my old man.

I unbuckled my seatbelt and got out the car, appreciating the light breeze. The temps had dropped about fifteen degrees and I was loving it. I activated the car alarm and rushed into the hospital's emergency room. I scanned the room until I spotted the Thompson twins, together in a row of bucket seats, holding onto each other. Their embrace made my heart constrict.

Love.

Before I could offer words of comfort, my cell made another loud declaration that I had another message. Niya's eyes narrowed with annoyance. Jazzy's expression mirrored hers.

Twins.

I ignored their glares. "How's Big?"

"Don't know yet," Jazzy replied.

Again, my phone dinged. "I'm sorry," I muttered and turned around to look at my phone. I knew better than to flash my screen this time.

Lakesha had sent another text. *Your son needs you to teach him how to be a man.* I clenched my jaw to keep from reacting since two pairs of eyes watched my every move.

Your son. Your son. If I heard those words one more time… I pressed the OFF button, shoved my phone into my pocket, and asked, "Anybody need something from the vending machine?"

Jazzy and Niya shook their heads in unison.

"You sure you don't want anything?" I asked them both again, but I had my gaze fixed on Niya.

"No, she don't want anything. Except, what she wants to know is when you fixing to tell her about your son?" Jazzy spoke up. Her neck snapped back and forth, causing her earrings to swing like a pendulum. "Can you go to the vending machine and come back with an answer to that question?"

I stepped back from her blaze-filled eyes. "Where you getting your facts from? I don't have a son." I tried to sound cool but my heart was moving faster than a rabbit being chased by a bobcat. Why did this girl have such a problem with me over stuff that wasn't even her business?

Niya rested an arm on Jazzy's shoulder. "Thanks, sis, but I got this." She stood and walked over to me. I told myself to play it cool.

"Lakesha's telling everybody you're denying your child." She cocked her head. "Why are you doing that? That don't even sound like you."

"There's no way that kid is mine," I said, pushing the flashing image of the physical similarities out of my mind.

Niya rested her hands on her hips. "So you didn't sleep with Lakesha?" Her face soured at the words.

Any response got caught in my throat. "Well, I, uh… It was a mistake and she intends to make me pay for it for the rest of my life, claiming that boy is mine." Another thought struck and my tongue loosened. "No doubt she heard I was into you and made this up to get back at you. Revive the rivalry."

Niya raised a brow. "Hold up. You making this about me?" Her neck snapped back and forth as she enunciated each word. "I can't believe you're twisting the story to suit your needs. No, your wants. You don't want to be a daddy."

"No. No, I don't," I yelled. "I don't want to be a daddy. Not now. Not ever."

Her mouth popped open and her brows shot up to her hairline. She stepped back. "You don't want children?"

I massaged my temples. *No, I didn't. Wait. Didn't I?*

Niya's eyes flashed but I could see the plea in their depths. "Answer me."

I swallowed. I couldn't. To answer would be to relive my childhood when I was done with my past. I lifted my chin. "Sure you don't want anything from the soda machine?"

"All right. Bet. Shut me out. Have it your way." Niya folded her arms. "After you help yourself to your snack, keep on walking. Don't come back here. We have enough drama going on with Big."

Jazzy came over to stand by Niya's side, like a sentinel keeping me at bay. My chest constricted when Niya buried her head in her sister's shoulder.

I took a tentative step forward. *Explain,* I told myself. *Say something or you'll lose your chance with Niya.* But my throat tightened.

"Niya, if I leave, how will you get home?" I asked instead.

Jazzy curved her body, holding Niya tight like she had to shield her from me.

"Niya, answer me," I urged.

"We ain't leaving Big," Jazzy spoke up, curling her lips.

Niya lifted her head to look at me. I saw the disappointment in their eyes and had to look away. I was no match against twin sisters united.

I trudged out of the waiting room feeling as if I had been pummeled to the ground by a sumo wrestler. I admitted I would've preferred a physical battle over the verbal tongue-lashing by the Thompson twins. They had won this round. My stomach tightened and I experienced a sunken feeling. Something told me I hadn't just lost a round; I had been T-K-O'd out the entire game.

8

NIYA

When somebody shows you their butt, you don't have to smell it to know it stinks. Despite my wounded heart, I chuckled as I remembered one of Big's analogies. Big had her own way of saying things. She said her sayings came from some time she'd spent with her Caribbean grandmother. "They got a saying for everything." She had laughed. "Phraseology."

Though I wondered how much longer I'd be able to hear her island wisdom, the memory of her words brought a smile to my face.

"What you laughing at?" Jazzy asked, huddled close to me. It had been close to forty minutes since Sean left and we were still waiting on word about Big's condition.

"Just thinking about Big, her phraseologies as she calls it," I said.

"I bet I know which one," Jazzy said. "Sean's butt sure was stinking tonight."

"Yep. Mr. I'm-a-Believer surprised me big time."

"Humph. Not me. To use another one of Big's sayings, the only thing *holy* about Sean right now is his drawers. Now, I don't know why she had a fascination with butts and undergarments but I have to admit, Big was spot on." She snapped her fingers. "Another Bigology that is truth: God is dropping Sean's pants and showing everybody the skid marks on his drawers."

I don't know if it was because I was scared of Big dying, but Jazzy's recollections broke the tension. Laughter bubbled up and overflowed. I clutched my stomach and laughed until Jazzy joined me. We laughed until we were both crying.

It took several minutes before we got our laughter under control.

I wiped the tears from my face. "I'm gonna miss Big and her famous sayings."

Jazzy got serious in a millisecond. She jabbed a finger into my chest. "Don't you start that nonsense. Big isn't dead."

"Yet," I filled in. "But one day, she's gonna be gone."

"Not today. She's tough," Jazzy continued. "Big has several more years left in her. She's too stubborn to go out that easy. Big would chase you with a switch if she knew you were giving up on her."

"I'm not. I won't." I clung to Jazzy's words with all the optimism I could muster. "You think we should try praying?"

Jazzy looked unsure but she nodded. "I don't know nothing about praying, so you go."

"I don't know what to say to God," I said.

"I guess you just have to—"

"Expose yourself to Him like you butt naked in the shower, 'cause He can see you anyhow," we both uttered. Another of Big's phrases. But this time, instead of laughing, I squeezed my eyes to keep the tears at bay. All my life, I had had Big. She had been my rock. The only constant in my life. Who could replace her?

I can.

I heard a whisper plain as day and scrunched my nose. *Who was that?* The voice sounded friendly, familiar.

Jazzy tapped my shoulder. "You plan on starting the prayer in this lifetime? Big needs you today."

I gave a quick nod and closed my eyes. There was no way I could tell Jazzy I was hearing voices. I cleared my throat. "Dear God, please don't take Big from us yet. We still need her down here. She's all we've had all our lives. Now I know You might be saying, me and Jazzy are grown now, but we still need Big." I lowered my voice to a whisper. "I know I don't check in with You like I should, but…" my voice broke.

Why would God even listen to this stupid prayer when He had professional prayers in His ear night and day? I forced myself to continue. "Please hear my prayer. I know I'm not good at it but I'm begging you to listen and hear the words from my heart."

"Mine too," Jazzy added.

I finished with, "Sincerely, Jazzy and Me, Niya. Amen." I sobbed. "P.S., I don't know how good this prayer is, but I hope You heard it anyway. Amen, again."

When I opened my eyes, I looked into eyes like mine, reddened with tears. My sister and I held onto each other and cried again.

"You did good," Jazzy said with a sniffle.

Dr. Mendez approached.

God worked fast.

We stood and my knees wobbled. I leaned into Jazzy for support.

"How is she?" Jazmin's voice trembled.

Dr. Mendez gave a wide smile. Any other time I would've zoned in on his stegosaurus-sized teeth, but today it was all about Big.

"Miss Thompson is a fighter," the doctor said. "She had a heart event because both arteries had serious blockage. But, I was able to clear the blockage and insert a pacemaker."

Heart event? I touched my chest and frowned. That sounded like a fancy way of saying heart attack, but I didn't want to confirm if my thoughts were true. My insides were already trembling something fierce at the words, "heart event".

"So she's going to be all right?" Jazzy asked, in a tremulous tone. We joined hands again.

Dr. Mendez nodded. "We're going to monitor her for a couple days, because I'm concerned about some blood clots in her legs. I don't want to risk a pulmonary embolism so I've put compression socks on both her legs."

"A pulmo what?" Jazzy asked.

"Pulmonary embolism," I supplied, my heart beating fast in my chest. I had never heard those words before and they sounded scary.

"Yes, that's correct," he repeated, nodding his head. "A pulmonary embolism, in simple terms, is when a blood clots form, usually in your legs, and travel to your lungs."

"Is that serious?" Jazzy asked.

His brown eyes held compassion. "It can cause a stroke or a heart attack," he answered in a gentle tone.

My sister and I looked at each other and gasped.

"But, she's okay for now," he said before looking at his watch.

I read that as his exit cue. Dr. Mendez was ready to move on to another patient or go home. "Thank you, doctor, for saving our grandmother's life," I said, though my chin wobbled.

He gave a brief nod. "Thank God. At the end of the day, it's all about Him," he said, pointing upward. "I'm just His hands."

Wow. For some reason, I didn't expect the doctor to believe in God. His words and humility impressed me.

"Can we go see her?" Jazzy asked, obviously not as moved as I was by Dr. Mendez's proclamation.

"Yes, you'll be able to see her once she's out of recovery and has been assigned a room in the Cardiac center. I'll make sure a nurse comes to get you when she's settled. But don't stay too long. She needs her rest."

As soon as he left, Jazmin lifted her chin. "I don't know about you but I'm not leaving Big. I'm staying right in the room with her until morning."

Jazzy was talking like she was the only one who cared about Big. I hated when she made it sound as if she was the only one willing to go the distance when it came to our grandmother.

"I'll be right there next to you," I said, steel in my voice.

"You don't have to stay," she replied. "I can call you if something happens. I know you're exhausted."

There she goes trying to spare me because she is a few minutes older. Jazzy seemed to think being born first made her the boss over my actions. Normally, I would have been glad for the respite she offered, but the night had been full of new beginnings. It was time I helped out more.

I squared my shoulders ready to stand my ground. This wasn't about Jazmin trying to get credit for taking care of Big, it was about me almost losing one of the few people dearest to me on earth.

"I'm staying," I said with even more resolve than before. "You're just as exhausted as me. If you can make the sacrifice, so can I."

"This isn't a competition," she pointed out. "I'm doing this because I love Big."

"I love Big, too," I said, emphasizing each word. "And, I'm not competing. I'm helping."

Jazzy relaxed and kissed my cheek. “Okay, we will stay together.”

I smiled. “I love her, too, and I…” I stopped before I broke down again. “I’m just glad she’s here. I’m thinking how I took Big for granted and I need her to know I love her.”

“She’s knows, sis,” Jazzy soothed.

I nodded, grabbing onto her words like I would if I were sinking in quicksand. They were life to me at this moment. I snatched her hand in mine. “I love you, Jazzy. I know I don’t say it often enough, but I love you.”

Jazzy sniffled. “I love you, too. And you’re right. We don’t say it enough.”

We sat down to wait to see Big. It was almost two a.m. before a nurse entered to say we could visit our grandmother. Jazzy had fallen asleep on my shoulder. I had stayed awake thinking of Big, my life, and Sean. I wiped my face and tapped Jazzy’s shoulder.

She shot awake. “How’s Big?”

“You can follow me. I’ll take you to her room,” the nurse said, leading the way out of the waiting room. She walked and talked, “I don’t want you to be alarmed when you see your grandmother. She’s hooked up to a lot of monitors so you’ll see lots of wires connected to her. She’s also swollen after surgery. But, she is very much okay.”

I nodded, though I didn’t fully understand why the nurse was talking that way. I didn’t know she was trying to prepare us for what we would see when we entered the room. All I knew was when the door swung open and I got my first sight of Big on the bed, I fell to my knees, almost taking Jazzy down with me.

That wasn't my grandmother in there. Gone was the surety of her face. Even though she hadn't been in the best of health before the heart event, her face had always been strong and determined-looking, even when she slept. All I could see was a shell, a shadow of the woman she used to be. Her features were slack. Passive. Like she was resting. If she hadn't been my rock, I might have found this comforting.

I wanted my spicy, fussy Big back. But she wasn't there.

I cried because I knew that no matter what the doctor had said, the truth was Big would never be the same. The Big I knew was gone. Forever.

9

SEAN

"You got kicked to the curb faster than an ice cream cone melts in Florida heat." Mike chuckled, leaning back into the couch that had set me back a good four grand. "The relationship that almost never was. You better get to singing and dancing to 'Kiki, D*o* Y*ou* L*ove* M*e*?' like the rest of the world."

I bit my cheek to keep from answering because I knew any response I tried to provide was going to sound not only weak but also pitiful. I also ignored Mike's reference to some song I didn't know. I related to William McDowell's "Wrap Me in Your Arms" and wouldn't be ashamed to say I could use a hug. But Mike was too busy with the jokes to show me any empathy.

"I'm sorry I called you over here," I said through my teeth. That was my comeback.

"I'm glad you called because you and I needed to catch

up." Mike pressed the auto switch and the chair expanded into a recliner. "So when did you and Niya become an item?"

I sat in the loveseat across from him. "I don't even know if you could call what we are an item. Yet." I refused to talk about our relationship in the past tense. I knew Niya was the one for me, knew that since forever, and I was patient enough to wait until she got the same message.

Mike lifted a brow. "You're optimistic."

"When you're sure about someone, you have no choice but to be. And, I'm sure my feelings for Niya are the real deal. She's the woman God has for me."

He held up a hand. "Whoa. I didn't know it was like that."

"Yes, it is like that," I said. "That's why I want to know what happened between the two of you."

This time Mike lifted both hands. "Nothing went down. Nothing worth talking about anyway. I tried to kick to her but Niya wasn't having it." He rubbed his chin. "I don't know why. I know I'm quite the catch, but I never even made it to the game with that one. She sure is fine though. And smart. I just settle with admiring her from afar. So you're free to see, my man."

My shoulders sagged. I was glad to hear that nothing had transpired between them. It would've been too messy for my taste but that wouldn't have stopped me. I was that sure of Niya's future role in my life.

"Thanks for coming straight with me," I said.

Mike shrugged. "Wasn't much to say." He cocked his

head. "So, do you plan on calling Lakesha and straightening out this whole situation with your son?"

"He's not my son," I shot back.

Mike raised a brow, daring me. "How do you know that?"

I averted my eyes. "I feel it in my gut. There's no way I could be a father and not know it."

Mike eyes bulged. "You're denying a child based on your gut?" He shook his head. "I'm not buying that nonsense, and you're way too intelligent to believe that crap. There's one sure way to find out," he challenged. "Take a paternity test."

I shook my head. To take a paternity test was to open myself up to the possibility... No. I wasn't going that route. I was quite content to swim the Nile, ignoring the truth of crocodiles threatening to swallow me whole.

"What for?" I voiced aloud. "Paternity tests are for those with questions. I don't need any answers. I don't have any doubts."

"You're a chicken," Mike said, his voice filled with contempt. "Turning your back on a child is a real punkish move. I would never have expected that from you."

I felt smaller than a fruit fly but I kept my back straight. Mike's disappointment hung over me like a rain-filled cloud. I wanted to continue to stay under my umbrella of denial. It was real shady under here. Sort of like me.

I shifted, not liking that feeling.

"A child is not a convenience or in this case, an inconvenience," Mike continued. "The boy is not an item in the store you pick up, change your mind, and then return to the shelf. He's a human, with feelings. And, he doesn't deserve this. He doesn't deserve you."

Those last words struck a nerve. I jumped to my feet. "You're right. He doesn't deserve me." I paced. "That boy doesn't deserve someone who doesn't know a thing about raising a child." I faced Mike, meeting his gaze. "You think I want to abuse him the way I was abused? You were there. You know what Pop did to me. You think I want to inflict that on another human being?" My chest heaved. "He's better off without me."

Mike stood and came over to place a hand on my shoulder. "What if you're all he has? What then?"

My heart stopped for a second. I swallowed then stiffened. "He has his mother." But even as the words left my mouth, I knew I had spoken a lie.

Mike knew it too. His eyes narrowed. "You think Lakesha is equipped to raise a man? I know society is all about the independent ladies but it takes a man to raise a man. Especially a black man capable of navigating today's world. If your son grows up to be a menace, you'll have yourself to blame. Because you took your golden opportunity to shape a life and buried it under your own selfish pride." His hands flailed. "Do you know how many of us I've had to put behind bars because of absentee, deadbeat dads leaving the women and children to fend for themselves?"

Absentee. Deadbeat. Those were not the adjectives I wanted to follow my name.

"You're right," I whispered. For the first time, I saw Lakesha's son not as hers but as mine, as ours. I saw RayRay's face and my heart cracked. I sucked in a breath, realizing this was my first time thinking of RayRay as my son. I looked down at my feet. Could I live with myself if he ended up behind bars, dead, or even worse, killing someone else because I rejected him? I knew the two-letter answer to that question.

My eyes filled and I faced Mike. "You're right," I admitted. "I'm being selfish. It's all about me. I don't want to go to Niya with baggage. I wanted to have my first child under the sanctity of marriage."

"Well, you didn't," Mike said without sympathy. "So, get over it and help your son."

"Yes." I nodded. Shame poured over my being. "I think I'll give Lakesha a call. I owe it to myself to at least find out the truth."

"You owe it to him. Little man needs you."

Mike's words seeped into my heart and I felt it expand. I straightened and scrolled to Lakesha's text message and hit the dial button. She answered on the second ring.

"Uh, hi. I was calling to arrange a time we could talk and I could meet with RayRay." I hated that I sounded tongue-tied but fatherhood was new to me. How did one meet the son he never knew?

Lakesha sucked her teeth. "No need to bother yourself. You think I'm going to wait forever for you to decide you ready to be a father and reach out to your son? Is that how you think this was going to play out?" She rambled like a run-on sentence, not waiting for my response. No commas. No periods. Lakesha answered her own question and kept going with the one-sided conversation. I put my phone on speaker so Mike could hear. "No way no how, somebody gonna play me like that. Someone else is taking your place. Yessir. Willie is more than happy to spend time with RayRay. So he won't need you to do him any favors. Willie is taking him for ice cream tomorrow. What you got to say about that?"

Mike's eyes were as wide as I'm sure mine were. "Wh—Who? Which Willie are you talking about?" I finally managed to ask.

"Willie Haynes."

Unease hit my stomach with the force of a boulder hitting the ground.

That cannot happen.

I knew God's voice.

Then Mike's reaction confirmed it. His mouth dropped. "No. No, dude," he mouthed.

"You can't be serious," I sputtered. "I don't want Willie Haynes anywhere near my son."

"Your son?" Lakesha bellowed. "Ain't this something. Now he's *your* son. He wasn't your son five minutes ago, so why does this even concern you?" Thankfully, she paused, giving me the opening I needed to answer.

I hurried to formulate the right words before she decided to continue her tirade. "I know I did wrong and I didn't handle the news well. But I needed time to come to grips with being somebody's father."

"Humph. Well, my friend, this is a case of too little, too late. RayRay don't need you and as for me, all I can say is good riddance."

Panic rose within me. I bent closer to the phone. "Lakesha, please don't let that man near my—I mean your son. I am begging you. Willie's got issues."

"How do you know that?"

"As soon as you mentioned Willie's name, God spoke to me. You don't want him near your child."

She snorted with laughter. "God's talking to you now? You mean to tell me God didn't tell you what you were doing was wrong? Or, do you only listen to Him when it's convenient or what you want to hear? Some kind of Christian you are, running from your responsibility." I hated that I had caused her and my son pain.

Mike covered his mouth to keep his laughter from escaping. "She read you," he mouthed again.

Her voice broke and I heard sniffling, like she was trying not to cry. "I didn't make this child by myself."

Lakesha wasn't biting her tongue. But I listened beyond her. I knew God was chastising me and all I could do was accept it. "I wasn't listening to God's voice before, but I'm listening now."

"Well, it's too late. If you want a relationship with RayRay, you're going to have to wait in line. Behind Willie.

He's a real man. He stepped up when you didn't." Lakesha cut the call.

I held the phone in my hand, mystified. What had I done?

Mike spoke up. "Willie isn't a real man. He's a suspected pedophile."

My feet almost gave way. "What? How can you know this and not arrest him? Why is he free to walk the streets if he's messing with kids?"

Mike rubbed his chin. "Because we have no solid proof, only suspicions. But from high school, I knew something was off about him. Word is, somebody from Willie's family—an uncle or cousin or somebody—sexually assaulted him as a kid. I don't know if the rumors were true, but I've had several calls about Willie sitting in the park watching the kids play. Technically, there isn't anything wrong with that and I have no proof so all I can do is ask him to vacate the premises." He shook his head. "I haven't found the glove that fits so I must acquit. But in my mind, he's guilty as sin. It's just a matter of time before I get him though." Mike cleared his throat. "Willie's done well for himself financially. After his father died, he had the good sense to use that insurance money and invest in a laundromat and dry cleaners. That's probably how he met Lakesha. Everybody and their momma be in his joints."

I sunk to the couch, overwhelmed at Mike's words.

I, too, remembered Willie as a weirdo. He didn't have friends or girlfriends. Instead, Willie hung by the bathroom at Lovetown High. I don't know what he was doing in the toilet stall, but the second stall on the second floor should've had his name on it. At graduation, I remembered how shocked we were to learn Willie had achieved a perfect score on the SAT.

"He should've taken that scholarship to Yale or Harvard," I said, voicing my last train of thought, knowing Mike would follow.

"Yep. He sure was smart. But no matter how smart he is, nothing negates the fact that something is wrong with Willie." Mike slapped his leg.

"I agree…" My stomach clenched.

Now Willie was sniffing around my son. I didn't want my son to be the bait trap. But I didn't want anybody else's son used to lure him into the open either.

"This is my fault," I said. "If I hadn't…" I trailed off, unable to voice the guilt rising like lava in a mountain.

"It is your fault," Mike replied, which didn't make me feel better. "So, if I were you, I'd figure out a way to fix it."

I dropped to my knees. "I think it's time I prayed." I looked at Mike. "Will you join me?"

He nodded and slid to the floor beside me. "I'm willing to try anything to snag a pedo. Even prayer."

10

NIYA

For the past two nights, Jazzy and I had suffered through sleeping in hospital chairs, twisting our torsos like gymnasts, hoping to settle upon a comfortable position. That never happened. And Big's room was cold despite the three blankets each the nurses had given us.

Big went in and out of consciousness. When she was awake, she recognized us. We saw it in the way her eyes scrunched in the corners, like she was trying to smile. But almost as soon as she started coming back, she'd slip into another deep round of slumber.

Now it was Monday morning. A weekday. Time for people to get back into a regular routine and start taking care of business. Not that Jazzy or I were much a part of "regular" life, seeing as we didn't have regular jobs or school.

It was kind of weird, when I thought about it. Was this the way I wanted to live the rest of my life, with no difference between a Saturday and Monday? Nothing to do all day except watch television, play games on my phone, and scroll through social media posts? When I was in high school, I liked the idea of doing nothing all day. But now that I'd been doing it for almost 10 years, it was...boring.

I hated to admit it to myself, but I liked being out of the house for a few days, even if it was because Big had this "heart event." This morning, we showered in Big's bathroom and gobbled down a couple of dried-out muffins from the cafeteria, despite the inconvenience, I welcomed my temporary "home". There was always something different going on, something happening. So far, the hospital had been a bustle of nurses and doctors and a hot-bodied technician who came in to run some kind of test on Big. Jazzy had flirted with him for a few minutes before they exchanged numbers. She'd been texting him off and on for about 24 hours now.

I rolled my eyes knowing that wouldn't last. Jazzy was dead set on finding a real life hero like the ones she read about in her ever-present stack of novels, and she had yet to find him. I'd told her many times to come back to reality but she was too caught up in her book boyfriends to pay me any mind. That didn't stop me from teasing her.

"Looks like you've made a new friend," I drawled out. "Got you a *doctor* with bulging biceps."

Jazzy blushed. "If you must know, Pratchett is a sonographer," she corrected me. Her eyes were zoned in on her phone as she tapped away at the keys. "And he's sleeping at the moment so you can quit your antics."

I stretched. "Who you texting then?"

"Cousin Glory Jean. She and Poochie are parking. They should be here in a minute."

I shook my head. "Oh my gosh. Why did you even tell them? Now they gonna come in here with their ratchet behavior."

"Big *is* their cousin. They should know what's going on."

I pressed, "Where's Glory Jean gonna stay while she's here?"

"I guess somewhere in the hospital. Pratchett said he could probably bring in one more chair if we'd like."

One more chair wasn't going to help the situation. Cousin Glory Jean was...well...Cousin Glory Jean. And that still didn't account for where Poochie, her daughter, would sit.

"What kind of a name is *Pratchett* anyway?" I asked her. "Sounds like a fancy golf club case."

"It was his great grandfather's name," Jazzy rattled off as though she'd known this fact all her life. "They're from California."

"People aren't *from* California. People might *move* there, but pretty much everybody in California claims another state," I told her, not to be outdone by her knowledge of Pratchett, who was probably lying about his background. I'd bet twenty dollars if I had it, he was from some podunk town in Alabama or Louisiana, trying to sound like he hadn't grown up in the hood.

"Knock, knock," a young, female voice called as the

door to Big's room opened.

Both Jazzy and I sat up. Big opened her eyes and turned her head to face the door.

"Hello, Ms. Thompson and family. My name is Kirstie. I'll be your nurse for the day." She turned her back to us, her long Senegalese twists swinging as she moved. Kirstie erased the name of the previous night's nurse and wrote her own in the appropriate spot on the dry erase board.

I couldn't speak for Jazzy, but I was sitting there in shock. We'd seen nothing but middle-aged white women come in claiming to be nurses.

Kirstie was black, and she couldn't have been more than 25 years old. She looked like someone who could have been one of our friends with her thick, filled-in eyebrows, gold hoop earrings, and a cross tattooed on the back of her left hand.

She smiled at us showing bright white teeth. "You must be her granddaughters."

My twin did the honors. "Yeah. I'm Jazzy. This is my sister, Niya."

Kirstie shook our hands. "It's nice to meet you both." She walked toward the sink near Big's bed and washed her hands. Then Kirstie checked Big's monitors. She recorded something on the computer and asked, "Has she eaten today?"

"A little," I replied.

"That's normal, given her condition. But if you two could get her to eat half of her breakfast, that would be great."

Kirstie finished up her typing and then asked, "Do you have any questions?"

"Ummm…" Jazzy ventured, "you a *real* nurse?"

A quizzical look crossed Kirstie's mocha brown face. "Ummm...yeah," she half-mimicked Jazzy.

Jazzy rolled her eyes, "If you say so." She smacked her lips and gave her attention to her phone again.

Kirstie continued. "I went straight to college after graduating from Lovetown High. I've been a nurse for two years now."

"We graduated from Lovetown, too," Jazzy said under her breath.

I added the numbers in my head. *Graduate at 18, go to college for four years, two years of working.* "So you're twenty-four?"

"Yes," she answered.

Jazzy abandoned the conversation, but I was intrigued. This girl was younger than me and already had a job. A *real* job. An important job helping people. And if she went to my old high school, she must have been from my neighborhood, too.

I blurted out, "How did you get in college? And how did you pay for it?"

The door to Big's room swung open wide and my Cousin Glory Jean rushed in. She wore a long, oversized plaid shirt, jeggings, and a pair of Jesus sandals. "Oh Lord, Lord, Lord have mercy."

The drama begins.

Jazzy and I rose from our seats.

"Cousin Glory—" Jazzy tried to calm her without success.

My cousin dropped her large world map purse on the floor, threw her hands in the air, and pushed past my sister to Big's side.

"My poor cousin." Cousin Glory Jean leaned over Big, staring into her face, like she expected Big's eyes to pop open and revive at the sound of her voice. When that didn't happen, she barked, "Is she in a coma?"

"No, ma'am," Kirstie answered, moving toward the machines, which forced Cousin Glory Jean to step out of the space nearest Big and give my grandmother some room to breathe.

I smiled to myself, thinking how clever it was for Kirstie to get Cousin Glory Jean to move out of the way. I wondered if they'd taught Kirstie that maneuver in college.

"She's sedated," Kirstie offered. "But in the next several hours, she should be able to communicate with you for a little while." Kirstie surveyed the machines again and entered another note on the computer.

Poochie arrived, breathless as a result of the trip from the car to Big's room. Poochie was my second cousin. She was in her late 40's, not too much older than my mother would have been, but she moved like she was the oldest person in the room due to her large size. "Hey, y'all." She huffed, wiped the sweat from her brow, then dried her hand on her navy blue broom skirt.

I wrinkled my nose in distaste, not wanting her sweat on me. But I got over myself and offered a hug. "Hey, Poochie."

Poochie lifted a hand to stop me. "Maybe later. Once I cool down." She turned left and right. "Is there a chair I can sit in?"

Jazzy pointed to the one she'd been sitting in moments earlier.

"I said a chair *I* can sit in. Not you, Miss Skinny Minnie." Poochie tried to tease, but her eyelids were heavy with embarrassment.

Upon second glance at Poochie's girth and that chair, I had to agree. She was right. There was no way she could fit more than half her butt in that seat.

Kirstie volunteered, "I can get a more suitable chair for you." There was no hint of judgment in her voice, which was more than I could say for myself. Maybe college would make me a more empathetic person, too.

"Thank you," Poochie said, looking down at the floor. Her long locks fell over her face, hiding the "most beautiful eyes we had in the family," according to Big. Poochie had grayish-green eyes. They'd looked like jewels to me when I was a child.

Kirstie left in search of a chair.

Breathing heavy, Poochie excused herself. "I'm gonna go to the waiting room. I'll be back."

That left me, Jazzy, and Cousin Glory Jean alone with Big.

"Now, tell me again how Big just upped and passed out,"

my cousin demanded with a hand on her hip.

"I was talking to her about college. Then, she was just...unresponsive," I explained. Somehow, saying those words took me back to that dreaded moment. I hoped I'd never have to repeat the story again.

"We tried to wake her," Jazzy picked up, "but she was out. So we called an ambulance and—"

Cousin Glory Jean interrupted, "What had she been eating?"

I shrugged. "Just regular things, like she always does."

"Y'all ain't overfeedin' her a bunch of junk lately, are you?" she clipped out, accusation lacing her words.

Jazzy reared her neck and swayed to one side. I knew my sister well. She was about to tell Cousin Glory Jean she had no right to question what we were feeding Big for the last two days on account of whatever she had been feeding Poochie all her life. I put a hand on Jazzy's arm and jumped into the conversation.

"She eats like she always has," I clarified. "Nothing's changed."

"Uh hum. She under more stress?" Cousin Glory Jean probed, narrowing her eyes.

"Not any more than usual," Jazzy said.

Kirstie returned, half-dragging and half-pulling a heavy, wide bench. I rushed over to hold open the door.

"Thank you," Kirstie said as she pushed the bench under the television, the only open space left in the room that might allow Poochie to sit comfortably.

"No, thank *you*," I said, knowing my tone held a lot of admiration for the younger woman.

"And you was worryin' her about college?" Cousin Glory Jean gestured for me to continue without acknowledging the nurse.

"We were *talking* about college," I said, slightly irritated.

"Well, that's probably what did it." She lifted her chin high enough so I could see up her nostrils. "Big ain't got no money to be puttin' you through school. It took everything she had to raise you two after your momma and daddy died. You think she wanna take on more responsibility and use a cut out of her social security check so you can give it to white folk at some *college*?"

I sucked in a huge gulp of air.

Jazzy fixed her lips and I knew she was about to say something crazy when, suddenly, we all heard a moan come from Big.

We all shuffled closer to her bed, including Kirstie.

Softly, she whispered, "Stop."

Kirstie asked us to step outside. "The last thing she needs is stress right now so maybe you can talk outside this room."

"That's what I'm tryna say," Cousin Glory Jean exclaimed, putting a hand on her chest. She shooed us out.

I pursed my lips. I'd had enough. My cousin was too extra for words.

Jazzy grabbed my arm. "Let's go to the waiting room." We left Cousin Glory Jean to fawn over Big.

Once we were in the hall, Jazzy fumed, "I swear, if it

wasn't for Big, I'd stomp on Cousin Glory Jean's bunions." Her voice carried down the hall, causing us to get a couple of wide-eyed stares.

Jazzy and I broke out into laughter as we entered the waiting room.

"I know you ain't talkin' about *my* momma." Poochie's voice came from inside the waiting room. We had forgotten Poochie was within earshot. Big's room was only a few feet away. We entered into the small space.

Jazzy spoke up. "I'm sorry, Poochie, she just..."

Poochie attempted to lift her body to a standing position and tried to steady herself with the chair's arm. While she struggled, she fussed. "Naw. Keep ya apology. We done drove two freakin' hours to get here and y'all wanna threaten violence toward *my* momma." With a huff, she was finally on her feet and plodded toward us at a snail's pace, wearing the expression of a warrior.

"Really, Poochie?" I cajoled. "You know how they—your momma, Big, and even my momma was when she was alive. They could *all* get on our nerves sometimes."

Jazzy and I inched backwards.

Poochie made a circle with her arm, snapping three times. "Don't try to play me. Y'all both sittin' up in Big's house doin' nothin' with your life, livin' off her fixed income. While y'all tryna *stomp* my momma's foot, you need to be stompin' up a job."

"Do *you* have a job?" Jazzy spoke through gritted teeth. "'Cause from what I know, you haven't left the nest, either."

"I got my *own* disability check," she boasted.

"For what?" I tag-teamed.

"For my lymphedema, thank you very much."

The door creaked open. "Ummm...excuse me," Kirstie said, coming inside the waiting area. "Can you please lower your voices? You're disturbing our patients." She posed the question politely, but her tone said she wasn't having it.

Poochie shook her head and bunched her massive fists. "Y'all about to have two more patients in a minute."

"We're sorry," I said to Kirstie.

"Poochie, you need to calm down before you get us kicked out." Jazzy crooked her head toward the door. "Go on in with Cousin Glory Jean. We'll wait out here until y'all leave."

"We gon' be here all day." Poochie cut her eyes at us as she waddled toward Big's room.

"Fine," Jazzy agreed. "Since y'all are here, Niya and I will head out. We could use a break, but we'll be back tonight."

"Whatever," Poochie snarled as she made her way to see Big.

I repeated, "Whatever," though of the two of us, Jazzy was the fighter. She was the one who never backed down. I was her loyal sidekick, hoping no one threw a punch because then I'd have to jump in to help my sister. Now, I didn't like violence, but when necessary I fought dirty and delivered a mean jab. I just preferred peace.

"I gotta go to the restroom," Jazzy said. She pointed

toward Big's room once Poochie had disappeared inside. "That girl made me have to pee." My sister jetted out the waiting room to the restroom.

"You okay?" Kirstie asked, looking at me with pity in her eyes.

I scuffed my shoe on the floor, hating how ghetto we must appear, but I didn't want her pity so I grabbed up my final dregs of pride. "Yeah," I said, shrugging my shoulders. "It's all good."

Kirstie took a deep breath.

I did the same and welcomed the calm that came with oxygen.

"Your cousin is wrong, you know?" Kirstie said, placing a hand on my arm.

"Yeah." I snickered, misunderstanding her on purpose. "There's no way she could make hospital patients out of me and Jazzy."

Kirstie shook her head. "I'm talking about your other cousin. The one who was talking about college. She's wrong about the money. You went to Lovetown High, right?"

"Yeah."

"So you grew up in either Lovetown or Red Valley. Right?"

I nodded.

"Well, if you grew up in our neighborhoods, living off your grandmother's social security check and both your parents were deceased *and* you had no job, you might have been able to go to college for free, using grants. And whatever your grants didn't pay for, student loans would cover. So, you could've gotten your degree and a job paying forty, fifty, sixty thousand a year and find your way out like I did. Because Lovetown is about to be a ghost town, so get out while you can."

Forty, fifty? Sixty thousand a year? That's, like, five thousand dollars a month. Those numbers sounded like figures from a board game with fake pink and yellow money. I didn't know anybody who made that kind of money. Legally.

"But how would I get to school? I don't have bus money or a car?" I quizzed, cringing at how pitiful I must sound.

Kirstie nodded like she understood. "I didn't have any money either, but I lived off the refund from my loans and used it to get to school and buy my books."

I straightened. "Refund?" I said, feeling hope rise within me. Jazzy would spot the cash I needed to start school for sure if she knew I'd be able to pay her back.

She nodded. "Yep. Just don't borrow more than you need so you won't have any problems paying it back." She cocked her head. "I can give you the website to apply for financial aid if you'd like? You've still got time to get approved before the next semester starts."

Firecrackers shot off inside me. *Me. In college. Forty, fifty, sixty thousand dollars a year.* I could do a whole lot of good with that money.

"Yes, please. Tell me everything you know."

11

SEAN

"Lakesha, open up," I said, banging on her door for the fourth time before pressing my ear against the wooden door. I could hear her moving about inside. "I'm not leaving until you open the door, so you might as well answer."

The door opened with such force, I lost my footing and catapulted into her house with unsteady feet. I don't know how I kept from falling, but I managed to regain my equilibrium by grabbing onto the edge of the small kitchen table. The plastic table cover shifted along with a huge vase of fresh flowers.

I hoped those weren't from Willie.

"You did that on purpose," I accused, pointing at Lakesha while fixing the table cover and re-centering the vase.

"I sure did," Lakesha said, cutting her eyes. "That's what

you get for pounding on my door like you the police. What's wrong with you?"

My chest heaved as I struggled to catch my breath, all the while looking out for the little man. "I came to check on RayRay." My eyes swept the room, taking in the soiled curtains, dirty dishes, and a pot bubbling up on the stove. I wiped my face with the back of my hand. The air was muggy from whatever Lakesha was cooking and she didn't have central AC.

She popped her gum. "He ain't here."

I lifted a brow and gestured for her to continue.

She sighed. "He next door playing with Rolanda's son, Henry. I'll be calling him in for lunch soon."

I nodded, though I had no idea who Rolanda or Henry were. I was relieved RayRay wasn't with Willie. I looked at my watch since the one Lakesha had by the kitchen table was stuck at 12:15. It was almost 11:30 a.m. and I had just finished getting a much needed haircut. I kept my hair low on my head and made Tyrone take off about two inches. Once I was done here, I needed to stop by the hospital before reporting in to work at 2:00 p.m. for a meeting.

I was pretty sure Niya wouldn't want to see me. And I was half-afraid Jazzy might scratch out my eyes on sight. But I had to go back to the hospital to check on Big. For Jhavon. I owed it to him. However, I knew I had to come check on my son first. RayRay had to be a priority.

Lakesha jumped twice before reaching on top of the refrigerator to get the bag of hot dog buns.

"I could've gotten that for you," I said.

"It's all good," she said, dismissing me. "I've been doing it myself for years without you." She turned off the stove and the bubbles subsided, leaving the hot dog franks floating.

Lakesha made a point of reaching for a bag of potato chips, sealed with a huge paperclip, and prepared two plates. I bit my tongue to keep from pointing out that RayRay needed proper nutrition. I didn't approve of their eating habits, but now wasn't the time to open my mouth.

I prided myself on eating right—most of the time—breaking my regimen only when Big cooked. Anything Big cooked, I ate. I wondered if Niya knew how to cook, then decided it didn't matter. I knew how to cook if she didn't. With Pop, I had to learn or I wouldn't eat.

"Why are you here?" Lakesha asked, brushing past me, annoyance evident in her tone. She moved the centerpiece to the coffee table in the adjacent living area and then placed the two plates on the table.

I squared my shoulders. "I want to be in RayRay's life."

"He has someone already." She opened the front door and yelled, "RayRay, come on and get your lunch."

I moved into her face to get her attention, then I emphasized, "I'm his father. He needs me."

"He doesn't need a father of convenience. He needs stability, not someone who will reject him one day and then try to claim him the next," Lakesha snapped back.

I winced. "I'm sorry for the way I acted, but I'm ready. I'm ready to have a relationship with him. I deserve the chance to do that." Even if I wasn't ready, I had to *make* myself ready in order to keep RayRay from falling victim to Willie. I would never let something like that happen to any child, let alone my flesh and blood.

She sat in the chair and I stood where I was since she hadn't invited me to sit. I didn't mind. I could stand for hours without a problem. The military and my father had prepared me well. Pops used to make me stand on one leg for hours.

I would never do that to my son.

I heard a light tap on the door and drew in a deep breath.

Lakesha opened the door and told RayRay to wash his hands. The little boy strolled past me like I didn't exist and walked down the main hallway. I gave Lakesha a look and cleared my throat, but all she did was open the refrigerator. It was clear she wasn't about to call RayRay out to mind his manners and acknowledge me.

I welcomed the blast of cool air. Sadly, the reprieve lasted mere seconds as she grabbed a jug of ice tea and closed the door.

"You want something to drink?" she asked, tapping her leg.

I took the olive branch. "Yes. Thank you."

Lakesha gathered three glasses and ice from a bag in the freezer. By the time RayRay had returned from the restroom, I was on my second glass of tea.

I chuckled. "This is tasty."

"Don't look so surprised," she said.

RayRay lowered his head and said grace. Seeing his head

bent and hearing his earnest words, my heart expanded. I knew coming here had been the right thing to do.

Thank God for guidance.

RayRay picked up his hot dog and took a bite.

"Hi, RayRay," I said, when it appeared Lakesha wasn't going to help with this conversation. In fact, she was steady eating her food.

"Hi," he answered, with too much attitude for a preschooler. But at least he answered.

I wiped my sweaty palms on my pants. I had no idea what else to say to him. My son. I walked to where he sat and bent to his level.

"I know I wasn't there for you in the past, and when you came to talk to me, I didn't say much, but I'm planning to fix that. You and me are going to be spending time together."

He kept his head lowered so I couldn't see his reaction. I noticed a tear roll down the side of his face. My heart squeezed, knowing I was the one who had hurt him, caused him pain.

I gave him a quick hug, ignoring the stiff shoulders. "I'm sorry I hurt you," I whispered. "I hope you'll give me another chance."

I felt his little head nod and my heart constricted. I stood and beckoned to Lakesha. We went outside, leaving the door cracked so we could see RayRay.

"I'll start paying child support," I said. "Let me know how much you'll need. And, I'll get him clothes, sneakers and supplies for school."

Lakesha's eyes lit up.

Inside, I revolted at her reaction.

"That sounds like a plan. There's these new Nike's I been meaning to get—I mean for him. Uh, and they were a hundred dollars."

I cocked my head. "Isn't that too much for a child?" I asked. "They grow so fast."

"Nothing is too much for my—I mean *our* child," she emphasized.

I nodded. "All right. I'll be by tomorrow with a check for you. And, then we can talk child support once the DNA results come back."

Lakesha stepped back. Her mouth opened and closed like a fish. "DNA results?" she hedged, then her attitude kicked in. "You think I'm a ho or something? I know who my baby daddy is. I don't need no DNA test to tell me that."

"You need to calm down," I said, holding up a hand. "Since you already know the results, what do you care if we take the test?"

She slid her gaze from mine and bit her lower lip. "I guess. But it's a complete waste of time. It's like you're already trying to get out of giving me my money."

"Hold up. *Your* money?" My voice held steel.

"Whatever," she said, with a shaky laugh. "I've got to get back inside. Call me when you coming by with that check."

Her sugary tone grated on my nerves. However, I held my tongue. Before I could say goodbye to RayRay, she closed the door in my face. I looked up to the sky and groaned. "God, I don't know if I can deal with this woman." Why had I gone there? I discerned Lakesha was going to be trifling, trivial, and as annoying as a fly in my ear. I trudged away, bemoaning the fact that I was the one who made a son with her. A son who needed me in his life. I couldn't swat them out of my life.

I hurried to my car, shifting gears.

Now that I had started the healing process with my son, it was time to tackle the other important person in my life, then check on Big. I pulled out of the complex and made the U-turn to head to the Lovetown Medical Center.

The entire way, I ignored the question churning through my mind. *What if Niya was finished with me forever?*

12

NIYA

I'd never admit out loud, but I was real happy to see Sean enter the hospital room. He was dressed in a navy blue suit with black shoes, which meant he had to be on his way to work. I bit the inside of my cheeks to keep my smile from busting out. After the way I had spoken to him, I didn't think he'd have the guts to show his face again. My heart had been in protest from the time he walked out the door two nights before.

I checked him out from under my lashes, admiring his fresh cut and shape up.

Sean held a bouquet of flowers I knew he had purchased from the gift shop on the first floor. I had eyed them earlier, wanting to brighten Big's room, but couldn't afford to spend that much money on flowers.

Jazzy rolled her eyes and stood. "I'm going to the bathroom and to get a cup of coffee." She brushed past him, freezing his greeting with a cold look. He was lucky she didn't throw the book she was reading at him, but knowing her, she wouldn't risk damaging the pages.

"Hey, Niya," Sean said, holding out the flowers. He looked uncertain...and cute.

I jutted my chin but declined to answer him. Sean didn't seem bothered by my unenthusiastic greeting. His eyes were all on me. My body heated under all that scrutiny.

"Hi," I finally said, taking the bunch in my hands. I sniffed, appreciating the distinct smells of daisies and roses and rubbed my cheek against the baby's breath. "Thank you. They're beautiful." I couldn't look him in the eyes knowing I had told him never to come back.

"You can't get rid of me that easy," Sean said, as if he had read my mind. "The only reason it took me this long is because I had to make things right with Lakesha before coming here."

"Lakesha?" I squeaked out, swallowing my jealousy.

"Yes," he said. "I apologized to RayRay and told her I'd begin paying her child support soon." He looked at me as if waiting for a sign of approval. Well, guess what? I hated that Sean had a child with someone who wasn't me. Yet, he stood there smiling at me like a horse wanting a carrot.

"I'm proud you manned up to your duties," I forced out. "Did you ask her for a DNA test? You've got to be sure before you get all in and find out she lied to you."

Sean nodded. "You bet. Lakesha got all bent out of shape about it, but I need to see it in black and white." He touched his chest. "I know it here though. I feel so much love for RayRay already. I didn't imagine being a father would feel like this."

I closed my eyes to shield myself from the love shining in his eyes for his son. I felt left out. I didn't know what it was like to be a parent. Instinctively, I touched my womb.

Sean reached for my hand and held it against his heart. "I can't wait to experience these emotions with you. At least, I hope to one day."

A tentative smile was all I could manage after his heartfelt declaration. He was being pretty bold with his feelings while I was feeling confused.

"Shouldn't you try to see if you can make things work with Lakesha?" I asked. "Then you could give RayRay a happy family with both his parents together." My stomach tightened. That wasn't what I wanted at all but I had to ask. Better to bring it up now than have to face that possibility later.

He gave a quick response. "I know my life got complicated all of a sudden, but I have no interest in Lakesha. I'll be there for my son. Period. That's it."

My heart smiled and I relaxed my shoulders, clinging to his words. I needed the assurance they provided, though I would never admit that to him.

Sean moved closer to me. "I never wanted a baby mama. I wanted—want—a wife." He tucked a finger under my chin until I was gazing into his soulful eyes. "I want you."

"Me?" I breathed out. "What could I give you?"

"Completion," he said, without hesitation. "You fill my heart until it is overflowing. Niya, you're the one I think of when I get up in the morning and who I dream of at night. Why do you think I came back to this town? I don't have anyone here. Just you."

"Whoa." His confession overwhelmed me. It wasn't every day a small town girl like me got to hear words filled with such passion...and love.

Sean kissed the back of my hand. I felt his full lips and yearned to have them pressed against mine.

"I'm probably saying too much, scaring you off, but I can't hold back from expressing how I feel any longer," he said.

All I could do was look at him. Feast on the sincerity in his eyes. My heart was eating up every word.

"Please, don't tell me you gon' fall for that," Jazzy said, startling me. "That's like cheap romance novel lines 101."

I snatched my hand away and covered it with my other hand, but it was as if Sean's lips had been seared on my skin. His touch lingered, teasing my senses.

Jazzy placed a hand on her hip. "Y'all have only gone out on one stinkin' date. You've never even *had* a boyfriend. *And* he got a child already. Really?"

"I meant every word," Sean responded, not taking his eyes off mine. He lowered his voice and addressed me. "I know we haven't had much time to reconnect, but I've always liked you. It was awkward, though, since I was so close to Jhavon. And the timing was off with the age difference back then."

"Well, the timing is *still* off because right now, it should be all about Big," Jazzy chided, cutting her eyes at me. "She's fighting for her life while you're making googly eyes at Sean."

Her words stung. I folded my arms about me. "Are you accusing me of not caring about our grandmother?" I snapped at her.

Jazzy's eyes flashed. She pointed at me, anger dripping through her tone. "Big is hooked up to machines, sleeping most of the day. She struggles to stay awake and to eat. That's what should be at the forefront of your mind, not Sean," she said, pointing his way. "So yes, it seems like you don't care or you need to get your priorities straight."

Sean butted in. "No, it sounds like you hatin'."

Jazzy got right in his face. "What do I have to hate on? I don't want your sorry behind."

"Jazzy… Sean," I called out in warning. Neither of them paid me any mind.

Sean continued the argument. "You're jealous because Niya dares to love. Do you expect her to be with you forever? Like spinster sisters? You can't imagine you'll be inseparable, like Niya doesn't want a life of her own."

Jazzy gave a harsh intake of breath and her face crumbled.

I felt her pain like it was my own. I looked between the

two people I cared about and shook my head. "Y'all need to stop," I whispered.

"Besides Big, she's all I got," Jazzy's voice wavered. "I can't lose her the way I lost everybody in my family, including Jhavon."

My sister's words pierced my heart and I knew what I had to do. I ignored the guilt of my wanting to become a nurse and even daring to fall in love. I couldn't bear to see my sister's dejection. Never mind that Sean was talking some truths. I went on the defensive and rushed to my twin's side.

I ignored Sean's regretful expression and cleared my throat. "Sean, I didn't say anything about love just yet. You have no right to interfere with me and Jazzy. We've been together since *before* birth. There is no separating us. She's my best friend for life."

Jazzy wiped the tears from her cheek and eyed Sean, daring him to utter another word. I took Jazzy's hand in a show of solidarity, but I was also panicking on the inside. I was pushing Sean away for a second time. He might not come back for a third.

I breathed an internal sigh of relief when he didn't walk out the door.

Sean shook his head and spoke to me in a gentle tone. "I'm not trying to come between the two of you. I just want you to open your heart and make room for me. Your heart can do that. God made it that way. You can have us both. You can have anything you want. And, I know you want more."

I did want more. I wanted to tell him all about what I'd learn from the nurse. And I wanted to ask about the Bible that I'd taken to reading while waiting on news about Big. I felt the words threaten to bubble out.

However, once again, Jazzy chimed in before I could. "She don't *need* more. Everything she needs is right here."

"That's right. Including me," Sean said.

I massaged the back of my head. "You two are giving me a headache."

Just then Big moaned, ending the argument. The three of us scurried to her side, the argument forgotten.

"Big? Big? Can you hear us?" I shouted.

"Quit all that noise," she mumbled.

"What did you say, Big?" Jazzy asked, breathless.

"Big." I squealed. "You're awake."

Sean gasped, giving God a loud praise. "God, You're good. Thank you."

"Y'all are making too much noise and I'm trying to sleep," Big said with a loud yawn. We watched with bated breath as she battled to open her eyelids.

"You came back to us," Jazzy said, covering her face. This time it was tears of relief that fell.

My eyes were full as I went to hug my sister. We rocked together. I was too overcome to speak.

"Big, it's good to see you." Sean's face beamed. "Let me go get the nurse." He rushed out of the room.

"Where am I?" Big asked, pulling at the IV.

I placed my hand over hers to still her movements. "No, Big. You can't pull that out. Leave it in. You're in the hospital. The nurse is coming."

"I don't like being in hospitals." Big moaned.

"Good. Because I don't like you being here either," Jazzy said. "You have to behave so they will release you."

Big closed her eyes.

Sean returned with the nurse and doctor in tow. They asked us to leave the room while they examined Big.

Jazzy and I hugged and cheered in the hallway as we stepped outside Big's room. Sean sauntered down the hallway, probably to avoid another altercation with Jazzy.

From the corner of my eye, I saw someone approaching. *I hope that isn't who I think it is.* I pulled out of my sister's arms and dragged us to the waiting room to face the unwelcome visitor. And, she was not alone.

Jazz rolled her eyes. "I'm going back so I can be by Big the moment they finish." She looked the visitor up and down. "You got this?" she asked me.

"Yeah," I said, pointedly looking at Lakesha, who stood a couple feet away. This girl was maybe a buck-twenty-five soaking wet. I could take her down if I needed to.

Wearing a too-tight halter dress and run-over flats, Lakesha smacked her gum and came into my personal space. "I came to see Big. She done cooked for everybody in the neighborhood at least once."

Lakesha pulled RayRay close to her side. She had a small teddy bear in her hand I recognized from the gift store. That store was pulling in some serious profits today with its overpriced items.

I frowned. Was Lakesha being genuine? Or did she follow Sean over here. "Big just woke up," I said, feeling skeptical about her sudden appearance, all the while wondering why Lakesha was making small-talk with me. I knew everybody loved Big, but Lakesha and I weren't tight like that.

Lakesha's shoulders relaxed at my words and she did a little jig. "That's some good news. Won't He do it?"

I pursed my lips. Lakesha was so extra.

Now I wasn't a church going person, but Lakesha's praise sounded hollow. Like she was putting on a front. I made sure to keep all I was thinking off my face, though my rapid blinking was a dead giveaway.

Sean appeared from around the corridor. Lakesha's face lit up at the sight of him. I could see her salivating over my man like a pit bull eyeing a piece of steak. I bunched my fists, resisting the urge to snatch her braids out of her head.

"Hey, Little Man," Sean said, coming over to where we stood. He stooped to face his 'son'.

Sean hadn't acknowledged Lakesha and I smiled, relaxing my fists. Call me petty Betty but my heart sang at Sean's reaction.

RayRay lifted his eyes and gave Sean a wide smile. I scrunched my nose. RayRay didn't seem all that bad like Jazzy had described. Then again, Jazzy wasn't one to interact with children. She didn't have the patience.

Sean and RayRay started a conversation with Lakesha hanging back to watch them. She still hadn't ventured into Big's room, which further enhanced my suspicions. *Lakesha followed Sean here.*

Suddenly, an odd feeling engulfed me. I felt my eyes go wide. RayRay wasn't Sean's son. Maybe it was something I learned in biology class. Maybe it was that he reminded me of someone else in Lovetown. Maybe it was the smirk on Lakesha's face. I drew in a breath. He wasn't. He wasn't. As sure as I knew my name, I knew I was right. Those facial features did not belong to Sean. I chewed on my bottom lip. The question was, could I convince Sean before he got more attached to the boy?

Watching RayRay's bright face soaking in Sean's words, I realized I had another dilemma. RayRay would be hurt. Again. Uncertainty filled my being. Would the truth cause more harm than good?

13

SEAN

It took everything in me not to confront Lakesha at the hospital. Her showing up was no coincidence. I was sure of it. I don't know what Lakesha's game was but RayRay had a spot in my life. Not her. Niya was the only woman I wanted next to me.

"It may be hours before they let us in to see Big again. I'll be sure to give her the gift." I extended my hand to take the bear from Lakesha.

She jerked it back. "I can give Big my gift myself. I don't need you for that. I don't need you for anything except to take care of your shorty. Got it?"

Niya blinked as though she couldn't believe the drama unfolding. I couldn't believe it myself. *I know Lakesha wasn't trying to come at me here? In a hospital? Visiting Big?*

I drew several deep breaths. “Lakesha, we can discuss all this later.”

She rolled her hip to one side. “Why? You don’t want your son to know what kind of father he has? But I do. My momma taught me not to bite my tongue. Tell the truth and shame the devil.”

I took the bait. “Your momma *should* have taught you not to discuss grown folks’ business in front of kids.”

“Boy!” She took a step toward me and readied her arms to push me, but I caught them before she could make contact with my chest.

“Lakesha. Stop it,” I said.

She tried to twist her arms free of my grip. “Let me go.”

“Stop putting your hands on him,” Niya shouted.

I was glad Niya was present as a witness. I was in a position that could lead to an arrest and a record, fooling with this woman.

As soon as I relaxed my hold, Lakesha slapped me with her bag.

Suddenly, a sharp pain traveled up the back of my arm. “Ow.” RayRay’s little teeth clamped onto me. “Stop it. Now,” I barked out.

He immediately released his bite on my arm and stepped away. But he called himself giving me a warning with a loud grunt. “I ain’t gonna let nobody hit my momma again.”

His words struck me harder than Lakesha had done. I looked into his wide eyes, which had welled up with tears, and I released his mother. There was no telling how much violence and drama my son had already witnessed. The last thing he needed was to see his parents in a physical altercation.

"RayRay," I said, hugging him close. "I would never hit your mother. *No one* should be hitting your mother."

"Save it for the judge," Lakesha piped up and pulled my boy from me.

"No. You save it for the judge because both me and that camera saw the whole thing. So, you can quit your trifling ways." Niya pointed at the round, gray ball in the top corner of the waiting room.

Lakesha's mouth popped open. "Whatever," she said, once she realized her scheme had been foiled.

"That's what I thought," Niya said, snapping her fingers.

"I'll give Big her gift later," Lakesha announced. She grabbed RayRay's hand and stomped out of the room. She slammed the door, cinching a few of her braids in the door-jamb. She yowled, retraced herself, then released her braids.

I bit my cheek to keep from laughing.

Niya, however, had no problem cackling. "That's what you get."

Lakesha left again, this time leaving the door ajar.

My stomach muscles relaxed the further she walked down the hallway, until RayRay looked back at me with daggers in his eyes, stabbing at my heart.

I wanted to say, *I want to be in your life, but your mother's making it difficult,* but all I could do was swallow the pendulum of emotions swirling in my mind.

Niya tapped her feet. "That girl is off. Like, Lifetime-Movie-jilted-stalker off."

I chuckled. "I agree. If things continue this way, I can foresee a nasty custody fight."

Niya gave me a blank stare before she took my hand. "Let's go get something from the cafeteria."

On cue, my stomach growled, reminding me I hadn't eaten since that morning. "Definitely."

We joined hands and Niya led the way. She weaved her way through the building with confidence. During the short trip, I pondered Niya's lack of a response to my custody battle prediction. I wondered if she appreciated my willingness to step up to raise my son if necessary. I was defying the stereotypical deadbeat dad.

We entered the cafeteria and headed to the serving line. Niya grabbed a tray and I followed suit before scanning the choices before me.

There were days I appreciated my military training. And, today, eyeing the mystery meat on my plate, I knew I'd have no problem eating it. I requested double helpings of mixed vegetables and pasta.

Niya, however, looked at the meat sauce and crumpled her face in disgust. "I can't wait to go home and eat some *real* food." She chose the baked potato, topped with cheese, and a bag of potato chips.

I paid for our meal and we sat at a table near the back of the cafeteria, facing the entrance. I wanted to be prepared in case Lakesha had the nerve to return.

Without asking permission, I took Niya's right hand and led us both in giving thanks for the food. "Amen," we said in unison.

She took a fork-full of her potato and hummed in delight. "Either this potato is really good or I'm starving."

I nibbled a bite of my pasta and said, "You're starving."

She chuckled. "Might be pumped up on adrenaline still, too."

I nodded, gave her a grin. "You stood up for me back there. I thought you were gonna go ninja on Lakesha for a second. Had to make sure I was lookin' at the right twin."

Niya poked out her lips. "Girls like Lakesha are all talk… and they learn real soon how to lie."

My brows furrowed. "What do you mean by that?"

Niya shrugged. "I'm just saying." She added butter and sprinkled salt on the potato before putting a chunk into her mouth.

I leaned in. "What are you saying, Niya?"

She met my gaze head on before rushing out with, "I'm saying I don't think RayRay's yours. Lakesha is latching onto you like a baby koala bear on its mama's back and she has no plans of letting you go."

"Listen, nobody staying on my back unless I put them there," I said and I meant every word.

Niya lifted a brow and kept eating, looking like she knew something I didn't.

"What?" I asked. "Speak your mind. I'm not into the

guessing games." I finally dug into the food and began eating.

"As sure as I know my name is Janiya Renee Thompson, I know that's not your son."

My heart pumped at a faster rate. "How you know that?"

"I just know it," she said. She touched her forehead with her index finger. "I know it right here. Call it intuition. You must take that paternity test. Don't let Lakesha talk you out of it. Although, it's only going to confirm what I already know." She placed a hand on her chest and said with amazement, "Listen to me. I'm already beginning to sound like a nurse."

"Huh?" I scratched my head. "You're talking all over the place and I can hardly keep up." I pushed my now empty plate aside. "What's this about sounding like a nurse?"

Niya's eyes flashed. "Yes. I'm thinking about going to school. One of the nurses, Kirstie, is making serious money and she's helping people. I watched her work and I know I can do that."

I smiled, basking under the umbrella of her radiant enthusiasm. This was a place I wanted to stay always. "All right. All right. I'm glad to hear you sound confident but I've got to warn you, it's challenging. The nursing program is not a walk in the park. You won't have time to sniff daisies, you'll be studying hard."

She jutted her jaw. "I'm not afraid of hard work. And, studying's easy for me." Her eyes narrowed. "I thought you'd be happy to hear my plans. Weren't you the one encouraging me before? Why are you hatin' on me now?"

"I'm not—" My phone rang, interrupting the conversation. It was Collin Marshall, one of the men who had been under my command. I hit the talk button. "Hey, Marshall," I said, using his surname.

"Hey, Chief. Did you hear about Simmonds?"

"Nah. How's he doing?"

"He, uh, he's dead, man," Marshall said.

I stood, feeling my eyes go wide. "Wait. What?"

"Yes. Dead," Marshall repeated. "Sorry to break the news to you."

"What happened?"

"You know Simmonds was good people. He died saving some woman who was being assaulted by her boyfriend. Simmonds rescued her and gave the man a beat down. But homie had a gun and shot him in the back. Can you believe that?"

"Yeah, I can actually. I'm not surprised that Sincere died helping someone." Sincere was the nickname we all had for Simmonds.

I couldn't believe what Marshall was telling me, but this was beyond a prank. It had to be true. *I can't believe he's gone. I was supposed to call him the other week and I didn't.*

I walked a short distance away from Niya in a daze. All I could see was Simmonds' laughing face.

"Word on the streets is, that woman is standing by her

man. Ain't that something? He died saving someone who obviously didn't want to be saved."

My eyebrows rose. "Wow. But that wouldn't have stopped Sincere. You know he wasn't about to stand there and watch a woman get hurt. As he would say, his mama taught him right."

"Yeah, that was him," Marshall said. Then his tone changed. "I can't believe he's gone. Just like that; in a moment, life as we know can change. We're all flying out to Los Angeles tonight. Hoping you can join us. His mother isn't taking the news too well."

Troy Simmonds idolized his mother. Maizie Simmonds had been his world. The men had often teased him about it, but Troy would shrug and say, "She's the only woman who will love me unconditionally for a lifetime." There had been no arguing with that. His words had caused a few men to wipe their eyes, myself included. Then, Ms. Maizie had become all our mother when she'd started sending care packages for me and several of my buddies.

"I'll book a flight. If I can be of any help to her, just say the word." I shook my head, unable to picture Simmonds still, without life. "I can't believe he's gone." I ran my free hand over my head. "I'll be there by tomorrow evening."

"Good. I'll tell the other guys. When stuff like this happens, all I can think is life is too short to hesitate. You have to pounce when opportunity knocks and grab onto everything good that comes your way," Marshall said.

"You're right, man." I looked Niya's way. *Or grab onto*

someone good. Like Niya. I knew then and there I wasn't going to let her go. Ever. I ended my call with Marshall and scurried over to tell Niya my news.

"I'm sorry for your loss," she said, once I had filled her in. "When will you be leaving?"

I pulled up my phone to look for flights. "Tonight if I can catch a flight."

"Oh. Okay. I'll be here when you get back," she said, preparing to leave.

"No, you won't," I said, reaching to hold her hand.

Niya licked her lips. "I thought..." She shook her head. "Never mind..."

"You won't be *here*, because you're coming with me." Seeing her wide-eyed expression, I rephrased my words. "I mean, I'd like you to come with me. So, will you? Come with me?"

14

NIYA

Maybe I shouldn't have said yes. What about Big? And if I went, would that mean we'd end up doing something...sexually? Am I ready for all that? I pondered these questions, standing by the edge of my bed after Sean asked me to go with him to Los Angeles. We had already stopped by his place to pack his bags. My mouth had hung open when he had given me the grand tour of his apartment. It was beyond nice, and I had told him that several times before he took me home. He was waiting outside while I got my stuff together but Jazzy's words plagued my conscience.

Jazzy had cussed me out when I returned to the hospital room and told her I was leaving. "Really? You're just going to leave me to take care of Big all by myself over some dude who's already got a baby and a triflin' baby momma?"

My sister had a way of saying things that made me feel

as insignificant as a dust particle. Guilt churned in my gut until Big spoke up from her bed.

"Leave her alone, Jazzy," Big croaked out, taking a sip of water. "I'm gon' be fine, getting stronger every day. Ain't no need in her staying here on account of me. I ain't gon' be no trouble when I get home. Just gon' sit up and watch TV all day, same as I'm doing here. Same as before I got in here."

I gave Big a grateful smile for coming to my defense. "Thanks, Big," I whispered, wiping a tear from the corner of my eye.

Jazzy's left eye ticked and I could see the fire in her eyes. It was only out of respect for Big that my sister didn't continue her tongue lashing. Brushing past me, she stomped out of the room.

I took a deep breath before stuffing my sandals into the side of my suitcase splayed open on my bed. Big was right. This wasn't about her. Or Sean. Or Jazzy. This was about me getting my own life. My own identity. Besides, Jazzy was going to have to get used to me not being around all the time because when I started college, I'd be busy.

Still, Jazzy and I were twins. Weren't twins supposed to always have each other's backs? Be there for one another? Hadn't it been our mother's wish we'd always be together?

But I'd always wanted to go to Los Angeles—the Big L to the A. I couldn't *not* go. Plus, I'd be helping Sean. I had seen the devastation on his face when he was on the phone with his friend, and I knew I wanted to be there to comfort him.

Speaking of comfort, I snuck my sexiest underwear I had inside my suitcase that afternoon, along with my razor and shaving cream. Sean was saved and the likelihood of any dancing in the sheets going on was smaller than my pinky toe, but I had to be prepared. Just in case. My heart started to pump with fury. Not that I had much experience. All right, none below the waist. But, I shrugged, *You never know.*

I dragged my toe under the snag in the carpet while I contemplated.

"You still packing?" Jazzy asked, coming into the room. After I left with Sean, she must have taken a cab home to shower and pack a change of clothes. And to confront me outside of Big's hearing.

"I'm done." I huffed, trying to close the suitcase.

Jazzy eyed me with heavy suspicion. "How long do you plan on leaving me here with all the responsibility?"

"Sean told me to pack for a couple of days."

She scrutinized my bulging suitcase and threw back the top flap before I could finish zipping it. "That looks like enough stuff for a month."

"I'm not sure of the weather so I have to be ready." I struggled to get the zipper to budge. The striped roller bag belonged to Big and was old enough to be considered trendy and antique. I hoped.

Jazzy crossed her arms. "You sure you coming back?"

Despite her underlying anger, I heard the fear in her voice and drew her into me for a quick hug. "Of course, I'm coming back. My life is here with you and Big."

Or, with Sean in that nice, spacious apartment.

I swallowed and told myself to calm down. I was getting way ahead of myself. "And are you forgetting that Sean lives around here, too?"

She crossed her arms. "He's been in the military. He's been all over the world. He could decide to move to Timbuktu or Dubai and take you with him."

"That's not going to happen," I said to reassure her. But I, myself, didn't believe my words. I was already planning to go to college and become a nurse. There was only one hospital for miles around. I would have to move out of my neighborhood to get a good job unless I wanted to drive, like, an hour a day back and forth to work.

Jazzy must have sensed the wheels churning in my head. Her next words were like a sledgehammer to my spine. "All I know is when Big does pass for real, don't you dare try to come acting like you cared, throwing your body all on her casket."

The very thought of losing Big made me choke up. "Don't say that." My chest heaved from the impact of Jazzy's words.

"Well, what else am I supposed to say? The truth is that we don't know how much longer we'll even have her in our lives, and…" her voice broke. She had verbalized both of our biggest fear.

My brows furrowed. "What are you talking about?"

Her top lip quivered, which made my breath catch, because my sister wasn't the crying type.

"Jazzy, what are you saying?" I demanded.

"I'm saying if something else happens to her there's not a whole lot they can do, especially at her age. The doctor said she has blocked arteries but Big doesn't want surgery, a whole lot of doctors, needles, and medicines with side effects worse than the disease."

I covered my eyes and shook my head. "Wait. When did all this happen?"

"While you were outside the room having confrontations with Sean's baby momma and having lunch with your boo."

Her words bit into me, tearing into my heart. "I had no idea," I sputtered. "Why didn't you tell me?"

"How could I when you came back with news that you were going to LA?"

I stood still. In that moment, I felt like I was in one of those old cartoons with a devil on one shoulder feeding me bad advice and an angel on the other giving the exact opposite advice. I just wasn't sure which shoulder the devil was perched on.

"Niya, you're selling out," Jazzy stated as fact.

She was right. Maybe. I gulped, hoping the life I was buying was worth what my twin sister said I was giving away.

15

SEAN

I didn't expect such a lackluster response from someone who had never been to LA or who had never previously been on an airplane. I expected to see Niya's eyes bright with excitement but other than squeezing my hand during takeoff and landing, Niya had been quiet. Her attitude had been blah at best. She barely noticed any of the sights or commented on the hustle of the LA crowds or the blaring horns.

For the third time since we'd caught the Uber leading us into the city, I asked if she was all right.

"I'm fine," was the quick response. Which meant she wasn't.

I held back a sigh. Her downturned lips and sad expression testified something was wrong, but Niya wasn't volunteering any information. Normally, I wouldn't push but my heart couldn't bear to see the woman I loved hurting. And, yes, I loved this woman sitting next to me, looking everywhere but at me. I loved her more than ice cream shakes on a hot summer day. She was cool, refreshing, and excited me in ways I doubted I had the eloquence to express. But I knew now wasn't the time to tell Niya how I felt. I needed to wait for the right moment to tell her I loved her more than eternity. I was cool with waiting.

"Is it Big?" I asked, taking her hand in mine and using my free hand to turn her head in my direction.

Niya shrugged but I could see her wet, spiky lashes.

I lowered my voice so the Uber driver couldn't overhear my conversation. "Sweetheart, you've got to talk. I can't help if you don't tell me what's going on."

She turned toward me. "I'm sorry. I'm not used to having anyone other than Jazzy and she's mad at me for leaving. She's making it sound like I don't care about Big because I came with you to LA. She said Big could die and called me a sellout for wanting a better life."

"Oh, baby," I said, pulling her under my arms. "Big will be okay. You said yourself that Big encouraged you to come. Jazzy is all in her feelings but she'll get over it."

When Niya rested her head on my chest, my heart expanded. I could feel the trust when she slumped against my chest, drawing strength from me, which made me feel seven feet tall. I would protect her with my last breath. I knew I sounded dramatic but what was more dramatic than being in love? Love had tilted my world off its axis. I so wanted to tell her but Niya needed comforting, I reminded myself.

Unaware of my inner conflict, Niya continued, "I would hate it if something happened to Big and she's all the way on the other side of the country."

A part of me wanted to blurt out I thought Jazzy was being selfish and was possibly jealous of Niya but I knew better. Niya and Jazzy were like peanut butter and jelly. There was no coming between them.

Thinking of them made me think of my friend Simmonds and the many hearty debates we used to have. No matter the issue, we were guaranteed to end up on opposite sides. I gulped. I'd never have any more. To me, Niya and Jazzy's arguments were inconsequential like a passing breeze in summer.

I gave her hand a gentle squeeze. "Nothing will happen, I promise. And, you and Jazzy will be fine. As long as she's breathing, Jazzy's going to argue. That's what she does but I know she loves you something fierce."

Like I do.

I kissed the back of Niya's hand and prayed for Big's recovery and to ease Jazzy's heart. Before I said amen, I couldn't resist adding a request for God to find Jazzy a man so she could have her own business to mind.

"We're coming up on the Staples Center," Lionel, the Uber driver, said.

Niya lifted her head and leaned out the window,

distracted by the driver's words. Her eyes went wide. "Wow. It's bright and sparkly, all lit up."

I had been to a few basketball games there but I, too, exclaimed like I was seeing it for the first time. "We'll have to come back another time and tour the town."

"That's where they had that rapper Nipsey Hussle's funeral. Traffic in LA is already bad but that day was a night-mare," the driver added.

I shook my head. "I can't believe after all these opportu-nities we have for progress, black folks are still taking each other's lives and fighting each other like crabs. That's why we can't get nowhere. We have enough people already against us, so we need to be united." I drew a deep breath and told myself to stop talking before I spooked the white driver. I noticed he had gripped the wheel with both hands once I'd started talking. It was a shame that even with my low buzz cut, polo shirt, and slacks, I could be seen as threat-ening or even intimidating.

Niya squeezed my hand and I gave her a small smile. Then the driver surprised me by continuing the conversation.

"I get what you mean, my brother," he chirped. "I'm Italian and we look out for each other. My family owns several pizzerias but I'm trying my own hustle after getting into it with my father. I'm about being my own man."

I relaxed. "I can relate. My father was... Let me just say he inspired me to be better than he was."

Niya touched my cheek. Her eyes were soft with compassion. I turned my head and swallowed my natural comeback of, *Don't feel sorry for me.* Instead, I allowed her compassion to wrap around the wounds of my heart and bring healing. I kissed the top of her head and whispered. "I'm good now. I promise you."

The driver fell silent and moved into the right lane toward our exit.

"Are we almost there?" Niya asked, holding back a yawn.

"Yes, we should get there by 7:30," I said, looking at my watch. We were about 10 minutes away from Ms. Maizie's house. I would be the last of the men to arrive. Marshall had already texted me that he and the other guys were there.

Niya yawned. "I'm pooped already."

I rubbed her shoulders. "Probably jet lag. And you've got to adjust to the time difference."

Her eyelids drooped. "By the time I do, we'll be back home."

"You just need a good night's rest and you'll be good to go. I know we're here for a sad occasion but I can easily get tickets to a game or something if you change your mind?"

I phrased my last word as a question. Niya had been insistent we didn't need to go anywhere. She was there to help me through my friend's funeral. But I hoped to persuade her to enjoy Los Angeles.

"No. You don't have to do that," she said. "Like I said, I came here to support you. I think you'll have to be strong for the other sailors and I intend to be your ride or die."

Her willingness to put my needs first increased my desire

to be everything and more for this woman. Niya had some rough edges but she was a diamond. I couldn't wait to help bring out that shine. I wasn't one of those guys who would try to bury that sparkle. I intended to gloss it up for everybody to see.

In less than ten minutes, we arrived at our destination. We thanked the Uber driver and exited the vehicle. I retrieved our carry-ons from the trunk. Niya brushed her hands across her white dress.

"We'll only be here about an hour before we head over to the Westin Bonaventure." That hotel had been the site for many Hollywood films. Niya would get a thrill out of that, especially since I had booked us a really nice suite. With separate bedrooms.

"We can stay as long as you need," she said, snaking her arm around my waist.

Together, we entered Ms. Maizie's house. I knew from experience it would be unlocked. I swear once I crossed the threshold, it was like I had stepped back in time. Everything looked the same. The sky blue walls and the huge portrait of Simmonds from first grade hanging in the foyer. I remember the first time I came here with Simmonds, I had teased him about that picture. I swallowed. We would never laugh again.

"Do we just come in like this?" Niya asked, interrupting my thoughts. "I don't want to get capped my first trip to LA."

"Yes," I said, with a small chuckle and took her hand. "It's cool." I sniffed. There was a distinct smell of charcoal in the air and my stomach grumbled. I hadn't eaten before our flight. "Let's head into the backyard; everybody's there. If I know Ms. Maizie, even though she's grieving, she's cooked up enough soul food to feed a fleet of ships." We entered the living room and I led the way toward the kitchen. There was a door that led to the backyard.

"I can't imagine she'd be cooking when her son died," Niya whispered. "If one of my family members died, I would be in my bed crying for days."

"People handle grief differently," I said. "When one of my cousins died, my aunt insisted on making, like, fifteen pound cakes. She gave them to everyone who came by for a visit because she said baking made her relax and feel like everything was still going to be all right."

Niya nodded slightly, as though processing a new way of thinking.

Marshall entered the kitchen, coming from outside, with a plate in his hand and stopped short. His mouth popped open when he saw me, but if I knew Marshall, he wouldn't be silent long.

"Chief," he shouted, placing his food on the kitchen island and lunging toward me. Niya released her grip on my hand.

Marshall and I hugged before I broke contact. His stocky build, red hair, and green eyes declared his Scottish heritage. I noticed his belly had rounded and jabbed him in the stomach.

"I'm so glad you're here," he said. "Ms. Maizie has been

cooking nonstop and none of us can get her to sit down. You've got to talk her into getting some rest. She's manning the grill. We've all tried to take over, but she refuses." Before I could answer, Marshall cocked his head toward Niya. "Who's this pretty lady?"

I sidled close to Niya. "This is my girlfriend, Janiya. Niya for short."

His eyes went wide and he took two small steps back. "Niya? Is this the Niya you were always talking about from your hometown? Your best friend's sister?" I could feel Niya giving me the side-eye, but I wouldn't look her way. Instead, I focused on the window with the wooden shutters I had helped Simmonds install.

I didn't care if she knew I had been talking about her for years, but Marshall reminded me how he'd earn the nickname, Strainer. I don't know how he made it far in the military talking like he did. He couldn't keep a secret past 24 hours. Make that 24 minutes.

Marshall tapped the bridge of his nose. "What was his name again? Your best friend?"

"Jhavon," Niya supplied, holding out her hand. "Pleased to meet you."

Marshall wiped his hand on his khaki shorts and shook her hand. I told myself to ignore the rip in his shorts and the newly added BBQ sauce stain.

"I'm Collin Marshall, but you can call me Marshall like everyone else," he said. "Chief told me all about your brother and how he died... It's a shame that—"

My stomach clenched. "Marshall," I interjected with a warning tone, "I don't think Niya wants to relive that history."

Marshall went red. "Right. Sorry about that. I just never imagined you two would get together. I mean, considering how everything went down." He shook his head.

Why would Marshall mention anything in front of Niya? The things my close military buddies and I shared—in those sweltering, endless hours during Navy SEAL training in the middle of a Louisiana swamp or in a Georgia forest waiting to be found after we'd failed a mission and been fake-killed —were things that shouldn't be repeated. Ever. Least of all now.

Niya winced. "What do you mean?" she asked.

God. No. Niya means too much to me.

I gave Marshall a warning glance and he coughed, realizing he was saying too much.

"I uh, I'd better go see about getting some ice." He grabbed his plate and rushed toward the door. I resisted the urge to bop Marshall on the head when he passed by me.

Once Niya and I were alone again, the tension rose between us.

"What did you tell him about my brother's death?"

"It was a long time ago. The details of what I told him are a little murky." Not true. I remembered every single detail about that night. Would remember them for life.

She pierced me with her glance. "But he said—"

"Jhavon's death was very painful for both of us. I shared

my feelings with these guys during some really rough times. And here I am, again, with another friend gone."

Niya's face changed into one of concern. "I didn't even think of it from your perspective. I can't imagine losing two close friends."

"Let's go meet the others and get you something to eat. The next couple of days is about Ms. Maizie and Simmonds," I said to Niya, holding out my hand. I held my breath and waited, hoping she would follow my lead. I couldn't have this conversation until we could talk in private and I could prepare her to hear what really happened the night Jhavon died.

Her eyes narrowed but she went along with the conversation shift. "We can talk about all that soon enough. You're right. This is about your friend." She placed her hand in mine. A sign of her trust. A trust I knew would evaporate if she knew the truth about her brother.

I gave a jerky nod and we made our way to the backyard.

"It feels good out here," Niya observed.

"Yeah. It pretty much stays summer until close to December. Then it feels like fall to me."

Her mouth formed an O. "Wow. I could get used to this, and it's not even that humid."

I smiled, admiring the light breeze teasing at her dress and hair. The temperature outside was about 82 degrees. Unlike Texas, where the heat could cause small sparks of fire on the asphalt.

There were mismatched chairs across the yard and about

six to seven men seated, eating burgers, corn, and barbecue chicken. Latin music played softly in the background. Ms. Maizie had her back turned, tending to the food on the grill.

"Why are you letting Ms. Maizie do all the work, you slackers?" I yelled, lifting a fist. "Hooyah."

"Hooyah," they responded, jumping to their feet.

My men swarmed me and I soaked in their warm welcome. I avoided Leroy "Bear" Holt's pat on the back. Bear had football-sized hands and I knew from experience he didn't always think about his strength.

Once we all had greeted each other, I introduced Niya to the men and made her a plate. I would eat later. Then I strode over to Ms. Maizie. She had turned to watch all the commotion and waited patiently as I made my way over to where she stood.

The petite, sprightly woman opened her arms, giving me a wide smile. A smile that didn't cover the sadness filling her blue eyes. "I've been waiting on you," she said. She had a few more crow's feet around the eyes and a little more gray in her curly hair but Ms. Maizie looked the same. Tears fell from her eyes and her chin wobbled. "My baby's gone. Just like that. My baby's gone. He's not coming back, is he? He's gone."

Fighting back my own tears, I shook my head. "I'm so sorry, Ms. Maizie."

Her knees buckled. I scooped her close to me to keep her from falling to the ground. Ms. Maizie shattered against me like glass hitting a concrete floor. I hoisted her shaking body in my arms, marveling at the sudden frailty of a woman who had been the energetic bee fluttering from one chore to the next.

Niya came over with napkins in hand.

"Let's get you inside," I said, using one of the napkins to wipe Ms. Maizie's cheeks. Ms. Maizie didn't argue which was a sure sign of her deep grief. I gestured to Bear to man the grill and I cradled her close. Ms. Maizie buried her head in my chest.

"I didn't want them to see me cry," she wailed before engaging into another crying session. It was like once her tears had started, there would be no stopping them. I was glad though because Ms. Maizie needed to release her pain. It was too much for her to keep on the inside.

"Never mind that. You go ahead and cry. No one is looking," I said loud enough for my men to look away. I began the trek across the lawn. Niya accompanied me and Marshall rushed to open the door.

I enjoyed the cool draft of the air conditioner and placed Ms. Maizie on the couch, still covered in plastic.

She grabbed my arm with surprising strength before her tears engulfed her. I sat on the floor facing her. Then I bowed my head and prayed. I felt Niya settle next to me and cherished her encouraging, "Amens" while I talked to God.

When I finished, Ms. Maizie thanked me. Then she asked in a tortured tone. "How am I going to bury my son? This isn't how it is supposed to be. Troy should be burying me. Not the other way around."

"I know, Ms. Maizie. But this is what God chose to do. At least we know Simmonds is in heaven."

Hope radiated in her eyes. "Yes. Thanks to you."

I bowed my head. "Thanks to God."

"I know what you mean, Ms. Maizie," Niya spoke up. "Sean's being humble. He's been talking to me about God and stuff, too. Because of him, my life is changing."

Ms. Maizie's eyes held curiosity. It appeared she was just now registering I had a woman with me.

"This is my girlfriend," I explained, aching to use another terminology. Fiancé was better suited and I intended to make that happen soon. But first I had to tell Niya I loved her.

"I can tell that you love him," Ms. Maizie said to Niya, who gasped and sat back on her heels. "I can see love all over your face. I know that look because that's how I felt about Harold. I never loved anyone else. He was my life mate." That proclamation led to another bout of tears.

Niya froze.

I knew the expression on my face could best be described as caught red-handed-holding-the-cookie-jar but I couldn't hold my shock. I don't know why Ms. Maizie put Niya on the spot like that. "She doesn't know what she's saying, Niya."

But Niya shook her head. "I disagree. She does know what she's saying." She bit her lower lip before looking me in my eyes. "And she's right."

Dang. Niya beat me to it. Kind of. Sort of.

My heart caught up. Wait. *Did Niya just say she loved me?*

I wanted to say, *I love you, too, Niya,* because my heart already knew it, but the words wouldn't come out. To this day, I have no clue why I sat there speechless when the woman I loved professed her love...kind of...in front of my deceased friend's mother.

16

NIYA

Did those words just come out of my mouth? I wanted to look down at my lips and ask them, *What are you saying?* But all I could do was put on a brave face after I had pretty much admitted to Sean I was in love with him though I hadn't uttered the three words.

Ugh... I knew better. I was old school. The girl was supposed to wait for the guy to declare his feelings first. However, my mouth had a mind of its own, blabbing what was in my heart. Now Sean might feel compelled to say he loved me, too. I frowned. That wouldn't count. How could I be sure it wasn't a pressure declaration and not true love?

Well… so far, his mouth hung open wide enough to catch a few fish and hold a loaf of bread. Five tense seconds ticked by and nothing. Nada. Zip. His silence was worse than a fake, "I love you, too."

I covered my face with my hand and mumbled, "Forget I said that." If I could have turned red, I would have. Ms. Maizie looked back and forth between us like she was at a tennis match, which only increased my mortification.

"Son, ain't you gonna say something?" she prompted Sean, which made everything worse.

It's like, if you have to ask someone for an apology, it's meaningless. I waved Ms. Maizie off, jumped to my feet, wiped my hands on my dress. I wanted to get out of this house, out of LA, and rush into Big's comforting arms even if I had to hear an "I told you so" from Jazzy.

I scurried out the front door and stopped on the porch. *Where could I go?* I heard the screen door slam behind me and straightened. Maybe I could downplay this whole situation. *Just be cool.* But that plan went awry when a tear escaped my eye.

"Niya, where are you going?" Sean put his hands on my shoulders.

"I needed fresh air," I lied, wrapping my arms about me and turning away.

"The air in the backyard is just as fresh as the air in the front yard," he reminded me.

Gently, he turned me to face him. I didn't resist, allowing him to see the tears trailing down my face. I stood there, open, raw, bare, knowing he would see my love shining through my eyes. I had opened the lid to my heart and I was woman enough to own my truth.

Sean's face melted and he pulled me into his arms. I inhaled the scent of his Joop cologne and waited for him to speak.

He spoke directly into my ear, causing shivers to run up my spine. "Niya, I love you, too." My body curled against him as he spoke words of love, feeding my heart.

"Wait." He pulled away from me and stared me in the eyes. "See? This is all wrong."

I threw my hands up. "What are you saying, Sean? I mean, do you love me or not?"

"I do, Niya. But this?" He looked around, gesturing toward nowhere in particular. "This was not how or where I wanted to tell you how much I love you. I mean, for years I wanted to go out with you, tell you how pretty you were. But I couldn't because...well...it's just not cool to be crushing on your best friend's little sister. So I had to be content with admiring you from afar. Our three years age difference was a big deal back then."

He smiled and I smiled along with him.

"Do you remember that time I got into a fight with Jerry Alderson?" he asked.

I rolled my eyes. "Uhhh...yeah. How could I forget? You two were rolling on the ground in the middle of the street like maniacs until Jhavon broke it up."

"Do you know why we were fighting?" Sean asked.

I smirked. "No. You guys were, what, sixteen? It could have been any reason. I don't even think people needed a reason to fight in our neighborhood. Especially not if it was with Jerry Alderson. He was weird. And a bully."

"We were fighting over you," Sean blurted out.

I stuck my neck out at his confession. "Me? Jerry Alderson liked me, too? Gross."

"Oh, he liked you all right. He liked you so much he was trying to use his expensive new binoculars his dad had bought him to look in your bedroom window. He bragged about how he'd seen you take off your jacket once and planned to camp out across the street from Ms. Jackson's front yard so he could see more."

Ms. Jackson used to babysit us and had been best friends with my mom.

My flesh crawled with this news as I pictured the line of vision from Ms. Jackson's to the bedroom I shared with Jazzy. My bed was closest to the window, and with the right angle, the right sunlight, the slight opening of the curtain, a pair of binoculars and a peeping Jerry, it could probably happen.

"The minute those words left Jerry's mouth, I grabbed his binoculars, threw them on the ground, stomped them with my Jordan's, and we started scrappin'."

All I could say was, "Wow."

"Yep. I dared him to tell his dad because I'd tell Mr. Alderson exactly why I broke 'em. I guess Jerry didn't want his old man to know he was a pervert because his people never called my people."

"Thank you," I said, placing a hand on his chest, appreciating the flex of his muscles underneath my palm. "Thank you for protecting me when I didn't even know I needed it."

"I will always look out for you, Niya," Sean said. "I did it then and I will do it now."

My insides buzzed. Electrical impulses shot through my being. I grinned, exulting in this sensation I identified as pure love. I could stay here all day but Sean wasn't done.

He licked his lips, sliding his gaze from mine. "When Jhavon died, it was…" He appeared to struggle to find the words. "I couldn't face you."

My stomach tightened. I came down from my love buzz. "What do you mean you couldn't face me? I mean, there was no reason to hide from me."

An awkward pause ensued. Enough time for me to take in the potted plants and the red bricks along the perimeter of Ms. Maizie's porch.

A cool breeze blew through us.

Sean shook his head. "Listen, the timing isn't right. I want to explain everything, but right now I don't want us to lose focus of why we're here." He cupped my head between his hands. "Just know I love you, Niya. I wish I could burst into the cook-out and shout, I love Janiya Renee Thompson at the top of my lungs but it wouldn't be right."

I chuckled. "I understand. I don't expect you to do that." I peered up at him from under my lashes. "I…uhm…I've never told anyone outside of my family members that I loved them. Ever. But the emotions just bubbled up from my heart." I searched for words. "Once Ms. Maizie said what she said, they had to come out, like an unexpected burp."

Sean's nose crinkled. "A *what*?"

We both busted out laughing. I scrambled to explain. "You know, like if you drink soda and then all of a sudden this—"

"Yeah, yeah, yeah, I get it," Sean said. "But you're saying that your love for me is like a burp?"

"Well, I haven't said the actual words yet," I reminded him.

"Don't," he said, putting a finger over my lips and pulling me back into his arms. "Don't say it. I want our first time to be special."

My knees gave way. All of a sudden, I wasn't thinking about the three words. I craved Sean's touch, his smell, his intimate ramblings in my ear. I wanted this man for always.

"It will be," I drawled out, my voice husky and filled with newfound desire.

"I didn't mean like *that*," Sean said, pulling away slightly. "I mean, when we make love we'll be married and it'll be special, but I was referring to the first time you tell me those words. I envisioned us going on a picnic, sitting on a red and white checkered blanket under an old oak tree."

Whoa. Sean must be reading Jazzy's books because that wasn't the way I saw that playing out.

"Uhm, Sean," I said. "I don't do outside. Or bugs. Or picnics. You've got the wrong chick in your fantasy."

"There were no bugs in my dream," Sean countered, pulling on my curls. "I've pictured this in my mind, in my dreams, for years. No doubt about it, Niya, it's you and me."

My lips curled into a smile. Something about the way he said it suddenly made his dream mine, too.

17

SEAN

Grief and sweat were not a good combination. I sat in the second pew on the hard wooden bench and resisted the urge to loosen my tie and roll up the sleeves of my white shirt. Niya sat beside me pumping the paper fan with fury. I told her it was better to sit still but she said she wasn't about to let her makeup run.

Pastor Long apologized for the heat a second time, wiped his face, and continued his eulogy. He had been speaking for about twenty minutes but his words were a blur. My face said I was listening but I would be hard-pressed to repeat anything he said. I was too distracted by Ms. Maizie crying in the pew before me. I wish I had the right words to comfort her. But what could I say when I didn't understand Simmonds' senseless death?

I swallowed my tears and looked around the room, listening to the sniffles and seeing the red eyes of many. Ms.

Maizie had asked me to say a few words but so far, I had nothing.

Niya dropped the fan. I reached down to retrieve it. "I can do that for you if you need me to," I whispered to Niya and wiped the sweat beads on the side of her face.

"I'm good," Niya said, giving me a small smile before turning her attention back to the eulogy. She cocked her head, furrowed her brows, and nodded along while Pastor Long spoke.

I snaked my arm around her waist and scooted her closer to me, needing to make physical contact despite the temperature. I was so grateful to have her here with me. I couldn't have done this without her. She curved into my arms and I took a deep breath. We fit together like puzzle pieces.

"He's calling for you," Niya said, squeezing my hand.

I blinked. Pastor Long had finished?

I stood and hesitated. "Lord, help me," I prayed.

"Just speak from the heart," Niya whispered. "You got this."

I nodded and released her hand before willing my feet to press forward. I gave myself a stern warning not to fall apart and walked up to the podium. I faced the two hundred expectant faces and all the tears I had swallowed rose to the surface. Acting on instinct, I lifted my hand and saluted the casket.

My men stood and joined me as we honored our fallen brother.

After that moment of silence, God poured words into

me. I cleared my throat and wiped my face. "No mother is prepared to bury her son. And, I am certainly not prepared to say goodbye to my brother. But God in His infinite wisdom prepared Simmonds to return to Him." I looked at Ms. Maizie. "Troy placed his life in God's hands. I was a witness to his transformation. The Simmonds before God was nothing like the Simmonds after God."

Ms. Maizie nodded. "He sure did change. One hundred percent for the better."

A few people chuckled despite their grief.

"Our nickname for Simmonds was Sincere." My voice cracked. "He earned that name because everything Simmonds did, he did from a place of love and sincerity. He was that person who went the extra mile and never complained. He would never find it too hard to help someone." I let the tears roll down my cheeks. "Even if it meant helping someone who didn't want that help. Because isn't that what God did for us?"

Through my blurry eyes, I thought I saw some heads nod. I zoomed in on Niya. "Simmonds is at home with God and I'm proud to have served our country alongside him. He was a fellow shipmate, a friend, but most of all he was saved by the grace of God through Christ. And for that reason, though I grieve," I gestured to the crowd, "though we all grieve, we can still smile in our hearts." I looked upward. "I'll be seeing you, friend."

I kept my eyes on Niya as I returned to my seat. She

thrust tissues in my hand before dabbing at her eyes. "That was beautiful," she choked out.

I touched her cheek. "You're beautiful."

Pastor Long announced it was time for the processional. I led Niya to Ms. Maizie and then went to take my place by the casket. A somber group of us took our friend to his final resting place behind the church. The congregation followed behind with Ms. Maizie surrounded by Niya, the pastor's wife, and her three sisters. Simmonds would be buried next to his uncle and father.

Emotionally spent after seeing my friend deposited six-feet-under the earth, I massaged my temples.

"Did you eat the banana and granola bar I gave you this morning?" Niya asked.

I shook my head. "I was too worked up to eat. I gave my snack to Strainer."

"Okay, we can get something at Ms. Maizie's house," she said, rubbing my back.

I scrunched my nose. "I've got a serious headache. I think I just want to get back to the hotel."

She cocked her head. "Are you sure?"

"Yeah." I jutted my jaw at the men surrounding Ms. Maizie. "She's in good hands. I doubt anyone will notice I'm not there. Besides, we have an early flight tomorrow morning and I did say goodbye to Ms. Maizie."

"If you're sure?" she asked.

I tapped on the Uber app. "I'm positive." My shoulders slumped. "I'm so exhausted, I can't even think straight."

Niya leaned into me and we held onto each other until the Uber arrived. Neither one of us felt like talking, and I caught a quick nap during the drive.

"Yo, you were straight up snoring just now," Niya said once we were inside the elevator of the hotel.

I leaned against the metal frame. "For real? I'm way more tired than I thought then." I swiped the key card and pressed the number eleven. The elevator took off with a swish. Within seconds, the door opened. I stumbled over my feet, bumping into Niya.

She grabbed my arm. "Careful. Follow me."

I emitted a loud yawn. "I'm sorry. I feel like I could pass out on the floor."

"Well, we can't have you doing that," Niya said, coming to a stop several doors down. "We're here." She pulled out her key card and opened the door to our suite.

Then she stopped.

And gasped.

Slowly, I straightened.

And smiled.

Niya's eyes were wide. She pointed to the large object propped against the couch before turning to face me. "You did this? Wow." Her forehead creased. "When? How?"

All I could do was nod. I was too busy grinning to articulate any answers.

She touched her chest. "Is this for me?"

"Of course, honey. Who else would it be for?"

She took tentative steps and walked toward the object,

holding back tears. "It's beautiful. I can't believe you did this. It's… I'm speechless. No one has ever done anything like this for me in my life."

By this time, my smile was ocean-wide. I ambled to her side to pick up the painting, holding it up mid-chest for her inspection. I needed to see every emotion on her Niya's face to record in my mind's camera. I planned to play back this moment over and over. I had managed to surprise Niya with a gift she would treasure forever.

Niya inhaled. With an air of reverence, she traced her fingers over the circumference of the artwork. I watched as she touched Big's likeness, running her finger across Big's cheek. Then she moved on to her and Jazzy. I watched her mouth widen with that beautiful smile of hers and my heart tripped. Seeing Niya's beaming face was worth every dollar I had paid the two artists to get this painting completed in days.

Then her eyes filled. "Jhavon," she whispered. Niya moved her cheek close to her brother's face. "I feel like he's about to come out of the painting and start talking to me. Oh, how I wish he could." Then she caressed my cheek with a look of such devotion that my heart forgot to beat for a second or two.

"I'm glad you like it," I breathed out.

"Like it," she gushed, eyes shining. "I love it. We always meant to take a picture together but then… Jhavon… Oh, thank you." Niya covered her mouth with her hands.

"I'll have the hotel ship it to your house so it doesn't get damaged during our travel home."

"Thank you." Niya did a little jig. "Wait till I show Jazzy and Big. I've got to take a picture..."

"I'll take it," I said, handing her the portrait. I took out my iPhone and snapped. Then I texted it to her. I waited until Niya sent her text to her family and placed the portrait on top of the coffee table. Then she wrapped her arms about herself and gazed at the painting.

I moved to stand behind her and hugged her from behind. Our bodies swayed, finding their rhythm, rocking together. My hands moved from her tummy to her arms. I turned her so I could look into her eyes.

Before I could say anything, she pressed her lips to mine. I forgot what I was thinking when her hands cradled my head. All I could think was I sharing my first kiss with Niya. Or, rather, she was kissing me. Her soft lips made butterflies zig zag in my tummy. My stomach clenched. I'd better take over. The painting wasn't the only thing she would remember about today. I was going to give her a first kiss she would never forget.

I pulled her flush against me and used my tongue to taste those luscious lips of hers. Then I sucked on them until she moaned and opened her mouth. I dove in to sample the treasure inside her mouth, taking my time. I don't know how much time passed before I released her.

Niya's long lashes closed and she exhaled. I held back

my grin. Oh yes. She had the look of a woman who had been kissed. I tucked her under the chin and she opened her eyes.

"Look at me," I said. "I love you. I won't get tired of saying it." Her mouth hung open like she wasn't sure how to respond.

Our chests heaved as our eyes did some serious talking. I observed her from under my lashes. Visual images of possibilities filling my mind.

I stepped forward. Her body language was telling me, yes.

But then the Holy Spirit spoke to me. *Retreat. Retreat.*

Niya bit down on her bottom lip. I groaned.

Just another inch, I told myself, picking up my foot.

Retreat, came the forceful tone.

I obeyed, finding my composure.

She squared her shoulders. "I love you, Sean Morrison."

All I could do was stare.

"What are you looking at?" she asked, looking up at me from under her lashes.

"I'm staring because I like taking my time to appreciate your fineness," I said. Then I took her hands in mine. "I will love you for an eternity."

"For eternity and a day," she added. "No matter what the future holds."

A part of me was so ecstatic, I could hardly breathe. My baby had declared her love for me. But the biggest problem facing me and Niya wasn't in the future. It was in the past.

18

SEAN

It was done. Niya and I were official. Together forever. I thought. I hoped. But I didn't rest well that night. Niya's love was sitting right on top of my heart, along with the confession I needed to make that might cause her love to dissipate.

But can true love do that? Can it leave in an instant? Or does it just morph into hate? I've heard old people say things like, "It's a thin line between love and hate," and "You can only truly hate what you used to love." Would it be like that between me and Niya once she learned the truth? Maybe I should leave all that stuff in the past and keep moving forward.

I tossed and turned, before throwing off the duvet cover. I rolled out of bed and got on my knees. Hands clasped, I prayed to God like He was my best buddy holed up with me in the trenches, ready to fight an unseen enemy at a moment's notice.

"God, I know I'm not perfect, but I try to live up to Your standards. Niya and I love each other and she looks at me with so much trust, I can't let her down with the truth of what happened to Jhavon. I don't want to tell her, but I can't live with myself if I don't."

I opened my lips but no words came out. I was stuck. Frozen at that last statement. *I can't live with myself if I don't.*

If I couldn't live with myself, I wasn't going to be able to live with Niya. Or Jazzy. Or the children Niya and I would have someday. Or our grandchildren. Everything would be built on a lie by omission, and Niya would feel as though I'd tricked her into thinking I was someone I wasn't. She'd take the kids and leave me, and I'd turn into a drunk old fool hanging out on a street corner singing that old song, "Used to be My Girl."

I buried my face in my hands, still kneeling before God. "How, God? When? Where?" I shook my head. "I don't know what to do."

My tongue loosened and I went deep into conversation with God, spitting out all my feelings to Him.

During my prayer, I felt transported back to my school days when the teacher told us if you explained the '5Ws' and 'how' in your research paper, the reader would understand your idea. Following that strategy, I had earned good grades on all my writing assignments.

That's when it hit me: That's what I needed to do with Niya. Be up front, answer all the 'W' questions and the 'how' so she'd understand my truth. I bunched my fists. I would do it. As soon as we got back home and settled into our new "us," I'd tell her everything.

I hunched my shoulders. "Okay, God. Thank You for the revelation. Give me strength." I stood and yawned. My body felt like it had been at the bottom of the train tracks. I trudged back into bed to get a few hours of rest.

"You got everything?" I asked as we checked out to catch an early flight back to Texas.

She mumbled something that sounded like, "Yes."

"Is everything okay?" I asked her once we were inside the Uber.

"Yeah. I'm not much of a morning person," she explained.

Somehow, that fact amused me. "Are you like this *every* day?"

She shrugged and leaned on my shoulder. "Pretty much. Takes me, like, an hour or two before I'm ready for conversation with people."

"Duly noted." I smiled almost the entire journey to LAX airport. My future wife was not a morning person. I'd have to show her the error of her ways.

Challenge accepted.

Though we were mostly silent, Niya and I moved in sync now, like the married couples I noticed in the airport. They stood next to one another, walked alongside one another, shared sips of each other's drinks, moving in and out of each other's spaces without a second thought. The only things Niya and I were missing were the wedding bands and the matching luggage. One day, however, that wouldn't be the case.

We navigated through the security-check line in under 20 minutes. Since we had some time before the flight departed, Niya and I sat in a nearby lounge after getting smoothies.

"Sean." Niya said my name in her sweet timbre, after finishing her pineapple-mango smoothie. "I need to talk to you," she said, her eyes darting back and forth across mine, fear written in the line between her eyebrows.

My chest tightened. I finished my drink. "What's up?" I gestured for her to speak.

She licked her lips. "I was looking at the picture of Jhavon again this morning and...for some reason...I thought about when Marshall said he couldn't believe I was with you after the way Jhavon died." She cocked her head. "What did he mean by that?"

My cheeks prickled with heat. *God, this is not the 'when' we discussed last night.* I cleared my throat. "Niya, it's...let's not talk about it right now."

She shook her head and looked at her watch. "I'm not going anywhere and neither are you for another hour." She touched my arm and added, "Whatever it is, I can take it." She chewed on her bottom lip. "Was my brother...involved in something we didn't know about? Did he owe somebody some money? Was he doing things—"

I had to interrupt. "No, no, Niya. Jhavon was as square as they come." My guilt intensified when her shoulders relaxed and she exhaled with relief.

"Oh thank goodness," she said, fanning herself. "Because I didn't know what to think."

I smiled. "Jhavon was everything you remember about him. He didn't deserve…" My voice came to a halt and I crumbled. Tears made warm trails down my face.

Niya squeezed my arm. "Sean, you're scaring me. What happened?"

I opened my eyes and faced Niya, knowing this might be the last time I witnessed love in her eyes staring back at me.

"Jhavon didn't deserve what *I* put him through."

Niya let go of my arm. I felt as though my pulse stopped without the pressure of her fingers wrapped around my wrist.

"What are you saying? What did you *do* to him?" She fired the questions at me with a distinct edge in her voice.

As bad as it sounded, I experienced a sense of relief with her accusation. It was time she knew and I would learn if she could still live with me after learning the truth.

I leaned into her space. "I didn't do anything to him. I couldn't. I mean, I wanted to help him, but I couldn't."

Niya squeezed her eyes shut tight for a second.

Help me, Lord. That was all I had time to utter before her eyes popped open.

She demanded, "Sean, start at the beginning."

19

THE NIGHT JHAVON DIED

"Dude, you stupid!" Jhavon laughed.

Sean flipped up the wrapper of a Laffy Taffy and looked for his next joke. He scanned the small paper and put his open fist over his mouth. "Aww naw. You ain't ready for this one," he yelled to Jhavon. "How do you get a baby alien to sleep?"

Jhavon shook his head and walked away from the candy aisle. "I can't with you, bro."

"You rocket," Sean yelled as though he were a comedian on stage with a coliseum full of people cracking up at his punch line. "Get it? Rocket...rock it!"

Old man Henderson, who owned the neighborhood corner store, teased from behind the counter, "If you're gonna read the jokes, the least you can do is buy some."

Sean grabbed a few pieces of his favorite flavor, grape, and joined Jhavon at the counter. He threw them into

Jhavon's pile of goods, which consisted of a grab-bag size of chips, soda, some gummy worms, and one of those *Black Hair* magazines. Sean didn't have to ask. He already knew the magazine was for Jazzy and the gummy worms were for Niya.

He wished he could buy the gummy worms for Niya, but then Jhavon would want to know why, and Sean would have some explaining to do.

"So you just gonna throw your candy on my tab, huh?" Jhavon asked.

"That's what friends are for," Sean said, slapping his best friend on the back.

Henderson scanned the items and announced the total. Jhavon paid for the items, telling Sean the next one was on him.

"I gotcha," he agreed.

"I'm a witness," Henderson joined in. "So, next time, you get the family size chips, right?"

"Right," Jhavon agreed, always eager to humor the old man.

"Naw, he will get that kiddie-size, right there." Sean pointed to the two-for-one dollar bags in the display near the register, the kind that only had a few chips in them. "And he's only getting one bag, not two."

"You two," Henderson laughed along with them, "you've been coming in this store since you were little boys. I've watched you two grow up. And your other two friends—Travis and Mike. You're all good kids. Stay away from all these hoodlums in the neighborhood. You hear? Y'all got plans to leave here, right?"

"Yeah, we'll leave," Jhavon said. "I'm going pro. But I'm coming back to make it better."

"Speak for yourself," Sean said. "It's every man for himself out here. When I leave, I'm not looking back." But even as he said those words, he couldn't imagine leaving Niya behind. He'd have to come back for her. For sure. He couldn't tell Jhavon that though. Not yet.

"Yeah, well," Henderson lowered his head, "come back or not, make something of yourselves either way."

"One hundred," Jhavon agreed, giving Henderson a fist bump.

Sean followed suit.

They exited the corner store, opening their goods as they left. Jhavon was chomping on his chips and Sean was just about to read off another joke when, all of a sudden, Flip and JJ came running from behind the liquor store at top-speed, their hoodies flapping in the wind. Moving off instinct, Jhavon and Sean turned around and took off running, because the way Flip and JJ were booking it, there might have been a pack of pit bulls coming their way.

Sean was about to grab the door handle and duck back into Henderson's store, when he felt his body being jerked away.

"Come with us," Flip demanded, leaving no room for argument seeing as Sean was literally off his feet at that point.

The next thing Sean knew, he and Jhavon were on the other side of Henderson's store, between the building and the dumpster.

Flip shoved a grocery-sized brown bag into Jhavon's chest. Jhavon grabbed onto it by instinct.

"You that basketball boy, always in the papers, right?" Flip asked.

Jhavon didn't have the presence of mind to lie. "Yeah."

"Hold this. Don't mess with it. We'll get it from you later."

And with that, Flip and JJ took off again, leaving Jhavon and Sean holding a bag full of God only knew what. They didn't have time to investigate because in the next moment, police sirens cut through the atmosphere. Jhavon and Sean panicked, running behind the store, hopping over two fences until they felt safe enough to sneak their way back to Sean's house, since it was the closest.

Hearts racing, they burst into the house. Sean had never been so happy to have a drunk for a father as he was that day. Pop was passed out on the couch, unaware his son and Jhavon had entered the house with a bag full of...what was it anyway? Dirty money? Drugs? Stolen goods? Guns?

Once inside Sean's room, the boys sat the bag on his bed and opened it. They gasped when they saw the contents inside.

Jhavon's shoulders dropped. He whispered, "Money."

Guns or hot clothes or even drugs might have been better. Those weren't everybody's flavor. But money? *Everybody* had a taste for money. The last thing they needed was for word on the street to get out they had a bunch of money stashed somewhere.

Sean pinched Jhavon's arm. "Why'd you take it?" he fussed, mindful not to wake his father.

"I didn't have a choice," Jhavon whisper-yelled back.

"We gotta give back that money," Sean said. "All of it. Flip and JJ, man...they're the *last* people I want looking for me."

Jhavon nodded. His eyes wide with fear.

Panting, they both stared down into the bag as if it held rattlesnakes.

"What's going on in here?" Pop screamed, stumbling into the room.

Sean and Jhavon jumped into action, blocking the older man's view of the bag. "Nothing," Sean said in a high-pitched voice, which caused his father to peer at them with suspicion.

"Y'all gay now?" he snarled.

"No, Dad. We been straight," Sean said. "Gon' stay straight for life."

"Well, I wouldn't be surpriiiiiised," Pop slurred, almost tripping over his feet. "You spend soooooo much time together."

Both boys were beyond Mr. Morrison's insults and had become immune to his verbal attacks. They kept cool, knowing they couldn't afford to get into an argument with Pop under these circumstances.

"We're best friends, Pop. You know this," Sean stated, enunciating each word like he was talking to a child. Why was he even trying to reason with a drunk, he wondered.

"I don't see you with no women," Pop pressed, wagging his head.

Sean lost patience. "Pop, I don't have time for this. Go back to bed."

"No, it's all right," Jhavon intervened, hedging toward the door. "I'll catch up with you tomorrow. Mr. Morrison, come let me out and lock the door behind me." Jhavon grabbed Sean's father's shoulder.

"Sean, I'll call you later," Jhavon threw the words back.

"Yeah. Your girlfriend will call you later." Pop laughed to himself.

Sean's stomach muscles loosened when his father complied. He watched Pop's zig-zagging gait with a huge amount of embarrassment laced with scorn. As soon as his father was out of sight, he tossed the bag far under the bed.

Sean got in the shower, wishing they'd stayed inside and continued watching movies instead of going for candy at Mr. Henderson's store. Why did they even go there anyway? Everything cost two times more than it would at Wal-Mart. And why didn't they say no to Flip when he asked them to hold the bag?

On second thought, Flip hadn't asked. He'd *told* Jhavon to hold the bag and there wasn't any declining. From what Sean heard, the last dude that told Flip no got hit so hard in the face his back teeth came out. Everybody in their neighborhood knew not to mess with Flip and JJ.

He washed his hair and face. All he and Jhavon had to do was get the money back to them, and all would be well. If Flip or JJ or anybody from their crew called, they'd return the bag, and ten years from now they'd be sitting around laughing about the night they got punked into holding a bag full of money.

As he finished showering, Sean's heart rate slowed. *This is not a problem. This is all going to work out.* Once he was dressed in a pair of black jeans and tee, he texted Jhavon but got no answer. *Where was he?* Sean told himself not to panic. *This is all going to work out.*

Later that night, Sean heard a light tap on his window and almost jumped out of his bed. He had sat in the dark for hours waiting and watching before drifting off. He glanced at his alarm clock—11:41 p.m. The neighbor's dog barked a few times, confirming someone was outside. His chest heaved. Was it Jhavon? Or, he gulped, Flip? Sweat beads formed while he debated, unsure if he should answer.

"Sean," a familiar voice called.

Sean released a huge sigh of relief at Jhavon's voice. *Thank You, God.* He slid out of bed and crawled to his bedroom window—couldn't be too careful—and opened it.

"Dude. I've been trying to call you," Jhavon whispered.

"What?" Sean asked in a hushed tone. He reached for his phone and noted the missed call notifications. "I turned my phone off because I didn't want to chance having my dad hear it and come in here. But, I thought I put it on vibrate. My bad."

Jhavon waved a dismissive hand. "Look. Flip's girl called. She said for us to bring the money and meet him behind Crowley's barbershop at midnight."

"Cool." Sean couldn't wait to get that money out of his life.

He slithered under the bed and grabbed the bag, then hoisted it out of the window at Jhavon, careful not to make too much noise. His father was nocturnal, drunk throughout the day but up at night eating meals and watching television. Somewhat sober, which tended to put him in a self-righteous parent mood, Mr. Morrison wasn't about to let Sean leave the house late at night. So, he'd have to sneak out for this mission as he had done many times before to attend parties or school-sponsored events.

Sean slid on a pair of sneakers and readied himself to join Jhavon on the other side of the window, when Pop opened Sean's bedroom door and switched on the light.

"What the—" Pop's mouth hung open.

Sean swung around to face his father. Jhavon ducked from sight but not before Pop saw him.

"I knew it." Pop snarled, bunching his fists. "You *are* gay. Sneaking that boy in your room." He made his way toward Sean with fire in his eyes. "That's sick. Disgusting." He struck Sean hard in his face.

"No. No," Jhavon yelled, "Mr. Morr—"

"Get off my property before I put a bullet—"

"Jhavon, go," Sean called. "Don't worry about me, just go."

Sean watched his friend scramble away and felt a sense of relief. At least they would be off the hook with Flip. He squared his shoulders, preparing himself to face his father, not knowing that would be the last time he would see his friend alive. That he had sent Jhavon to his death.

20

NIYA

My left eye ticked.

"Sooo, you sent my brother to meet up with the most ruthless thugs in the middle of the night all by himself? That's like sending a lamb to go meet up with some lions." I summarized Sean's sorry story. Dangerous volts of electricity coursed through my blood, stabbing me from the inside out. "You know as well as I do *anything* could pop off with those punks. That's why they call him Flip, you know? Because he flips all the way out over *any-little-thing.*"

Sean replied, "I know, and I was—"

I cut him off. "And you know my brother. You know that despite how scared he had to be, Jhavon was probably trying to talk some sense into them. They got jealous because he had a way out of our stupid town." I put a hand over my mouth as the terrifying image of my brother surrounded by a circle of Flip and his cronies plagued my mind. They came after him the same way kids taunted the shy kid on a playground. Only these guys were bullies with bullets. They harmed people for fun… "Oh, God," I choked out, caught up in the scenarios racing through my mind.

"Niya, I was going to go with Jhavon but my dad—"

"Why didn't you tell your father what was happening?" I questioned, cutting him off again.

Sean closed his eyes like he was praying for strength, then drew in a large amount of air. "He refused to listen to me." He shook his head. "You don't know my pop. Once he got something in his head, there was no telling him different."

"Okay, but when you saw you weren't going to make it to the spot and my brother was in over his head, you should have called the cops. Give an anonymous tip where my brother was going to meet those guys."

"No, Niya, I couldn't have," he denied, as though my suggestion was unreasonable. "First of all, the police wouldn't have come in two minutes." He held up two fingers. "And, if they had gotten there as it was going down, Flip would know I tipped off the cops."

"So you saved your behind and left my brother to face Flip and his crew? Why didn't you call Mike or Travis? Anybody? I mean, at least if there were two people, they might have had a fight on their hands."

"Niya, the whole thing happened so fast, I just…pshhh..."

My brows furrowed. Was that all he had? *Pshhh?*

I poked him hard in the chest. "And you're just now telling me this?" I shook my head. "How long did it take you to come with this nonsense, Sean? You let the police and everybody else in the neighborhood think my brother was involved in illegal activity, given the time of night and being behind Mr. Henderson's and all." I allowed all the contempt and anger I felt to be heard in my tone. "The way you left my brother's reputation in question...that's just shady and disrespectful."

"Nobody who knew Jhavon would believe that," Sean said.

It was true. Those closest to him knew better. But we hadn't been able to answer the officers' questions about why Jhavon was where he was when he died. And it had pained my heart to see how the news speculated on Jhavon's character in the absence of solid answers.

Yet another question popped into my head. My eyes narrowed. "How do I know you didn't set my brother up? Maybe you were jealous of Jhavon this whole time. Maybe you *wanted* him dead."

Sean's eyes bulged and his eyebrows shot up to his hairline at my accusation. But after what he'd just told me, I didn't know what he was capable of. If he could lie to me and my family for all these years about Jhavon's death, he had probably been lying the past several weeks. I lifted my chin. The way I saw it, Sean was never Jhavon's true friend.

Sean stood. "It's time to go. They are boarding now."

I refused to take his hand, following behind him in a

daze. Before I knew it, we were seated on row nineteen, buckled in, and ready to take off. Sean was seated at the window, I was in the center, and a tubby Asian man who hadn't wasted any time going to sleep had the aisle seat.

The pilot's voice came on the airplane's sound system.

"Welcome aboard today's flight to Dallas Fort Worth, Texas. This is your captain speaking. We expect to encounter some turbulence ahead, so please observe the fasten seatbelt signs throughout the duration of the flight. Flight attendants, please serve the snacks and drinks early and then remain seated as well. We're fourth in the cue for takeoff, as soon as we're cleared, we will cruise up to thirty-thousand feet."

Once the announcement ended, Sean whispered, "Don't shut me out, Niya. Please."

I ignored Sean's distraught expression, closed my eyes, and stiffened my spine in an attempt to shield myself from the avalanche of tears. Tears summoned by betrayal. My body shook with anger and waves of rage ripped through my heart.

For a moment, I experienced an out-of-body experience. Goosebumps spread across my arms. I saw myself strangling Sean. Squeezing the life out of him with my bare hands. He pulled at my fingers to pry them off his neck, but my grip grew tighter. Stronger. I killed him, right there in the airplane and no one could save him.

No one.

Whoever tried to stop me, I killed them. I strangled them all.

I frowned as reason weaved its way into my imagined world. My actions didn't make sense. I only had two hands. I could only strangle one person at a time. I snapped out of it and studied my hands, shivering with fright. The vision had been so real. I wiped the sweat on my brow and took sharp breaths to calm myself.

"Niya, are you okay?" Sean asked, shaking my shoulder.

Panicked, I reached up and pressed the button for the flight attendant to come. I pressed it again. And again.

"Niya, what are you doing?" Sean reached for my arm.

I jabbed him in the chest with my elbow. "Don't touch me," I lashed out. *I might kill you.*

"Ow," he said, in stunned disbelief, massaging his chest.

The flight attendant scurried down the aisle. Her purple lips held a wide smile. "You only need to press it once," she said, all sugary and sweet but her rapid blinking eyes told me she was annoyed. "How may I help you?" she asked.

"I need to change seats," I bellowed. Without waiting for her consent, I unbuckled my seatbelt and scooped my purse off the floor.

She placed a hand on her hip. "I'm sorry but you'll have to stay here. The captain has engaged the seatbelt sign. We'll be in turbulence soon."

"Ma'am, this guy confessed something that changed my world," I pointed at Sean. "If you don't move me from him, we're going to have a serious problem."

She looked at Sean. "I'll move if you want me to," he volunteered.

Shaking her head, the attendant muttered, “Lovers’ quarrels.”

“We’re not lovers,” I corrected.

Her purple lips twisted into a patronizing smile. “Come with me, ma’am. There’s a seat on row five. But you’re going to have to remain there for the remainder of the flight.”

“That is perfect.” I cut my eyes at Sean and pushed past the Asian man who dared to be sleeping with a serene expression on his face when my world had disintegrated. I retrieved my luggage, kept my chin up and followed the attendant to my new seat. After a quick, “thank you,” I hoisted my luggage into the overhead bin and squeezed my way between two larger women who huffed at my presence. I shrugged and settled in. I’d rather endure smelly armpits on my left and onion breath on my right—seriously, who ate onions on a plane?—than sit with someone who was my brother’s killer.

And, yes. Sean was my brother’s killer. His punk behind stayed home and left Jhavon to face the toughest dudes in our town on his own. He might not have pulled the trigger but he didn’t stop it either.

My chest heaved as I dissected Sean’s story. How could I make him pay for what he’d done? Then a thought occurred. How was I going to get home? I couldn’t afford Uber and I wasn’t getting into *his* car. I’d rather walk than endure another moment in Sean’s presence. I snapped my fingers and pulled out my phone. As the plane taxied toward the runway, I sent a quick text.

"Miss, please put your phone in airplane mode or shut it down," Onion Breath said to me.

"Please put your breath in check," I shot back. I covered my mouth, immediately regretting my words. I wasn't mad at Onion Breath and I wasn't trying to start a disruption. I was just mad and hurt and all in my feelings because of Sean. "I'm sorry," I said, contrite. "I'm feeling a bit stressed. I'm shutting it down now." I made sure she saw me power off my cell phone and slip it into my purse. All I could do was pray my text had been received.

Onion Breath pursed her lips and gave a small nod. From my side-eye, I saw her dip in her pocket and pull out a stick of spearmint gum. Thank goodness for that small reprieve. Now I could go back to thinking of ways to make Sean pay. I looked at my watch. I had about three hours. Enough time to think of the appropriate way to torture someone and get away with it.

I leaned back into the seat and closed my eyes.

It felt like minutes but I felt a tap on my shoulder. I opened one eye. "Yeah?"

"We're here. It's time to go," Onion, I mean, Minty Breath said.

That snapped me awake. I didn't even know I'd drifted off. "Oh. Thank you." I snatched my luggage and scurried out of the plane. I didn't want Sean catching up to me. I scuttled through the crowded airport, ignoring my grumbling stomach, snaking around sleepy toddlers and smartly dressed businessmen. My eyes remained fixed on the exit signs. I panted from exertion but I wasn't slowing down.

My cell rang. It was Sean. I pressed the END button.

It rang again. This time I answered.

"I'm here," he said.

"Thank you. Thank you. Thank you," I said. "I'll be right there."

Knowing I had a ride made me walk faster. I heard a shout behind me. "Niya. Wait up." I propelled my feet toward the exit and jogged to the waiting red Ford Explorer.

"I'm so glad you got my text," I said, struggling to catch my breath. I took a moment to savor the cool AC.

"No worries. I was just getting off my shift," Mike said. "And, you know I'd do anything for you."

I shifted. "This is the only kind of ride you'll have with me." I grabbed the door handle.

Mike held up a hand. "It's all good, Niya. I know the deal."

My shoulders slumped. "Good. As long as you know this is a favor. Nothing else."

"It's all good," he said. Just then Sean rushed in front of the car, and Mike slammed on the brakes. He lowered his window. "Yo, you trying to get yourself killed, man?"

"Niya," Sean called out, coming over to lean his head into the car. "Niya. I need to talk to you."

I folded my arms and looked at Mike. "Drive."

Mike raised a brow.

"Niya, please get out the car and talk to me," Sean said.

I hated how he was drawing attention to us. "Leave me alone," I shouted. "I don't ever want to see you again."

"Whoa," Mike exclaimed, holding up both hands. "What's going on?" He looked between the two of us with wide eyes.

"Mike," I said, through gritted teeth, "if you know what's good for you, you won't ask me any questions, you'll just drive. Drive the car."

Mike eyed me and must have realized I was serious before he said to Sean. "Step off, man."

"Niya, I need you," Sean pleaded in a hoarse voice before he backed away.

I looked Sean square in the eyes and spilled the wretched words from my heart. "I wish it had been you instead of Jhavon."

Mike took off.

I hated myself for doing it, but I glanced into the rearview mirror, allowing myself one last look at the man I loved.

No, I didn't. I couldn't love my brother's killer.

I closed my eyes and my heart, resenting the tears that dared to spill for a killer. But they had a will of their own. My lips quivered and my body trembled before a sob broke through.

Mike reached across me, his fingers grazing my leg. I froze before realizing he was opening the glove box. Mike grabbed the box of tissues and handed them to me. Then he turned the radio on, most likely to drown out the sound of my tears.

"Thank you," I said, grateful for his thoughtfulness. It had taken all my strength to be able to say those two words before my emotional dam broke. I turned my body away and leaned into the passenger window and cried.

Like a sad love song, it started to rain. I welcomed it. God was crying along with me. I cried the entire journey home. And, when I got into the house, Jazzy stood waiting.

She scanned me from head to toe before opening her arms. I rushed into her embrace and to my surprise, I had enough water in my body to cry more tears.

"What happened?" she asked, rocking me. "Where's Sean?"

I held my chest as my body heaved. "He. Oh God, I can't say the words," I said.

She stiffened and pulled away. "What can't you say? Niya, you're not making any sense and you're scaring me." She wiped my face and cupped my cheeks with her hands. "What is going on with you? Did something happen with Sean?"

I licked my dry, chapped lips. "He… He told me—"

"Wait," she said, dragging me to my feet. "Big needs to hear this."

I shook my head and dug my heels in. "I can't tell Big. It might…" My voice dropped. "It might… She might get another heart *event.*"

Jazzy hesitated before placing her hands on her hips. “Whatever it is, it can’t be that bad.”

I forced *his* name out of my lips. “Sean… It was Sean. Sean. Sean. Sean.” I screamed and pulled at my hair. “He’s responsible for Jhavon’s death.”

Jazzy shook me. “Calm down and talk to me.”

I nodded, took several breaths, and peered into Jazzy’s eyes that had gone dark and cold. Chilled, I rubbed the goosebumps on my arm.

“You’d better explain,” she commanded. “Don’t leave anything out.”

21

SEAN

"Why didn't you tell her *everything*?" Mike asked. He had been waiting in the parking lot for me when I got home. Without a word, I let him into my place and we went into the kitchen where I told him what had transpired with Niya.

I straddled the stool and sat by him at the bar-style kitchen table.

I shrugged. "I did tell her what she needed to know. It was my fault that Jhavon died."

"Your fault? Your fault?" Mike shouted, flailing his arms. "Your father beat you senseless. You crawled your way to the meet up because you wanted to help Jhavon."

As crazy as it might sound, I didn't want Niya to know about my father's severe physical abuse. I'd already seen her look at me as though I were a snake. It would have been all the more worse for her to see me as a weakling. Pity wasn't my goal.

Mike shook his head. "I don't get why you're blaming yourself. You're the one who's supposed to be saved. You know God controls life and death."

I balled my fist. "Then why didn't He take me?" I raged. "Why did He allow my friend to die? Jhavon had a basketball career ahead of him, but me, I was worthless. I wasn't worth the dirt under my fingernails." I lowered my head close to my chest. "No one would've cared if I died. Especially not Pops. Niya is right. It should've been me."

"But it wasn't," Mike said. "I can't believe you've been walking around with this guilt all this time. Brother, you've got to let this go."

"But I wasn't there," I sobbed. "I wasn't there."

Mike came over to where I stood. "I've seen many promising lives cut short while many evil ingrates survive. Flip and his thugs are big as ever and we're trying to bring them down. But that's another conversation. You were a kid, Sean. You did the best you could."

"And it wasn't enough." My shoulders slumped. I closed my eyes. "I lost my best friend, and now I've lost Niya. All because I was weak and…" I gulped.

"It was enough," Mike said, patting me on the shoulder. "God kept you alive for a reason. Your life has a purpose."

Tears rolled down my face. "Not without Niya. She's my rock. My everything."

"No woman can be your everything. You have a son. A legacy. Concentrate on RayRay. He needs you."

I rubbed the bridge of my nose. "I'm getting a paternity test. Niya urged me to get one done to be 99.99 percent certain."

"She's right," Mike said.

"Yeah… She's a good woman. She just isn't *my* woman anymore."

Mike stepped back. "Get a grip, brother. It's time for you to pray. You're making this woman cloud your judgment." He chuckled. "Why am I the one telling you this?"

I knew Mike was right, but all I could see was the hate on Niya's face. Her scornful expression was ingrained in my heart. I winced, feeling literal pain.

"You've got to seek the Lord since He's nowhere around," Mike said.

I lifted a brow. "I think you mean, Seek Him while He's found."

"Yeah." Mike shrugged. "Same thing. Do that and quit feeling sorry for yourself." He shook his head. "It's not a good look." He sniffed. "Or smell."

Despite my heartache, Mike made me smile. "Thank you, Mike. God is using you and speaking through you. I hope you know you can't run from Him forever."

Mike waved me off. "Uhm, let's stay on the topic of you. Now go pray and do what you do and win back the girl."

I did just that.

I prayed. I poured my heart out to God. I released the

guilt and pain I didn't know I still carried over to Him, asking for His healing. Then I tried to win back the girl.

I called. I visited. I called some more. But there was no getting through. For two months, I pleaded my cause until I received a restraining order. Then the truth sunk into my brain and weaved its way to the core of my being.

Niya was done with me, forever. And, there would be no changing her mind.

It was only because of my faith in God that I was able to press forward. I flourished at work, but on the inside, deep in my heart, I was a shell. A shell of the man I was with Niya. I recited the serenity prayer, which became my mantra. I said it all the time. I was actively being pursued to move to Washington D.C. next summer but I resisted. Because of Niya.

Niya. Niya. Niya. She filled my thoughts and dreams.

Then I saw her.

I had an appointment at the college to talk to some recruits. For a moment, I wondered if she was an illusion because of how much I had been thinking of her. But the woman scurrying across the lawn was very real.

She'd cut her hair and dyed it blonde but I would recognize my love anywhere. She had a stack of books in her hand. My heart pumped in my chest and my throat went dry. I looked at my watch. My appointment was in fifteen minutes. I needed to walk in the opposite direction to the administration office. But my feet had other plans. I propelled after her, running like there was a herd of elephants chasing me.

"Niya," I called out.

She stopped and faced me, holding up a hand. "You can't come within 50 feet of me. Why can't you leave me alone? I want nothing to do with you after what you did. Or *didn't* do." Her voice and eyes were Antarctica-cold, but I couldn't let that deter me. I figured I had nothing but pride to lose and even that was running on low.

"I know." I nodded. "But I have to talk to you. Please. I only need three minutes of your time to say three things." I held up three fingers. "Three minutes and three things and then you never have to hear from me again. You can call the cops on me after if you want but please just hear me out."

"A lot of good that's gonna do, since your best friends are officers in this town. Oh, wait—are they really your friends or are you planning to set them up, too?"

"Niya. Come on," I pleaded. "You *know* me."

She chewed on her bottom lip and adjusted the books in her hand but she didn't walk away. I used that as my cue to start talking.

"First of all, I'm glad to see you've started school. That's awesome. Second, I got the results of the paternity test and it turns out you were right. Lakesha is still denying it but I am positive RayRay isn't mine."

I paused, hoping to see a response but Niya remained stone-faced. I felt despondency seep in. Niya didn't appear interested in hearing anything I had to say. But I pressed on.

"Third, I love you more than life itself. I will never stop loving you. You'll always be in my heart. I intend to wait for you until eternity if I have to." My voice broke but I was glad I had spoken what I felt.

She met my eyes then and lifted a brow. "I've heard you out. Anything else?"

Wow. My shoulders slumped. I realized then it was time for me to cut the last shred of hope I had been holding onto in my heart. I took a step back. "No. That's all I had to say. Thank you for listening."

She gave a jerky nod and spun on her heels. Then she paused and my heart skipped a beat. But her next words crushed me. "Don't contact me again. If I never hear from you or see you, it will be too soon. You got that?"

I lifted my chin, summoning the shrapnel of pride I had left, despite the devastation that filled my entire being. "Yes," I whispered. "You've made your wishes crystal clear and since that's how you want it, that's how it will be."

I shoved my hands in my pockets and trekked across campus to my meeting. Without Niya, there was no reason to stay in Lovetown. I drew a deep breath. After my meeting today, I'd make a call. If Washington D.C.'s offer was still open, I would accept. Maybe distance would heal my heart and give me the power to move on.

22

NIYA

"You can't hide out in the house forever," Jazzy said, swatting at a mosquito. She'd nagged me into accompanying her to Mr. Henderson's, saying she had a craving for Funyuns. After five minutes of her pleadings, I had caved.

"I don't get why we're going to Mr. Henderson's. Ms. Mabel has Funyuns. You know I don't like coming here. You don't either, so I don't understand the sudden urge to go here." I avoided a crack in the sidewalk and held onto Jazzy's arm so I wouldn't lose my footing. "I don't know why you couldn't have waited until I changed my sandals."

Jazzy playfully pulled on my curls. It had grown a couple inches since my impulsive pixie cut and color.

"I couldn't have you changing your mind," she said. "I barely see you anymore and this is the first day I can leave the house since Big's aide started today." Jazzy had fought for Medicare to provide home health care so she could get much needed assistance caring for their grandmother. "You're so busy with school and homework, you don't have time for anything or anyone else."

Seeing the hurt in her eyes, I strove to explain. "Starting school after all these years is intense. I had to complete refresher courses in English and Math and then they had me taking chemistry and science courses. Those classes were kicking my butt big time so I had to study twice as hard. It's tough playing catch up."

Jazzy nodded, "I get it and I'm happy that you're going after something you want." My chest puffed at the pride in her tone. "Just don't forget about me."

"Oh, Jazzy," I said, taking her hand. "I told you to enroll with me. We could go together. And, I'll always have time for you."

"And, who would take care of Big?" she asked, giving me a pointed look. "If I wasn't there, Big wouldn't be alive."

"Don't you think I feel guilty that you're doing so much?" I asked. "Now that I'm on break, I'll be able to help more when I can and when I become a nurse I'll be of more help."

Jazzy nodded. "I know… I'm sorry for beefing at you, but I miss you. Big will have round the clock care and I don't quite know what to do with myself."

"You could write since you love to read so much."

Hope flared into her eyes. Then Jazzy shook her head.

"I'm good." She gave my elbow a playful jab. "You do it for the both of us."

We stopped at the light across the street from Mr. Henderson's store. The walk sign came on. I froze and grabbed Jazzy by the shoulder. "I don't want to go there."

"Come on," Jazzy said, tugging me across the street.

Once we were in front of the store, I paused. "This was Jhavon's store. Every time I go in there Mr. Henderson brings him up." I shook my head. "I just can't. Especially knowing what I know now."

"That's exactly why we're going in there," Jazzy said with stubborn determination.

I dug my heels in. "I should've known this wasn't about no Funyuns. You're going in there for information. I told you going after Flip and 'em is a big mistake. Ain't nobody going to ever bring those dudes down."

She jutted her jaw. "I can and I will."

A couple of boys came out of the store eating fruit chews and gum. Jazzy and I cut off the conversation. Flip's ears reached far in the neighborhood. They greeted us with nods and went on their way.

I waited until they were a little distance away before continuing. "Jazzy, stop this crazy plan of yours. I'm not trying to lose you, too." My lips quivered.

"You won't lose me. We are going to live way beyond seventy years old. Now let's go get my Funyuns." She took my hand and led me into the store.

"I don't know why we had to come here, though," I

mumbled under my breath. "Don't see why Ms. Mabel's wasn't good enough."

I headed toward the chip aisle but Jazzy kept strutting until she was at the counter. I frowned. What was she up to?

"Hey, Mr. Henderson," she greeted, batting her lashes.

I cocked my head and glared. Jazzy reached for a pack of gum and opened it. She took her sweet time, undoing the wrapper and popping a Bubble Yum into her mouth. I realized she was nervous and trying to cover it.

Mr. Henderson raised a brow. "You gon' pay for that?"

"Of course. I got more than enough to pay for it… and more," Jazzy said. A look passed between them. I wrinkled my nose. It was like they were having a whole other conversation.

Jazzy flipped her hair and reached into her short-shorts rear pocket. It's a good thing Big had been asleep when we left. Big would've carried on something fierce at the crop top and shorts even though she had a coverall.

My mouth dropped when I saw the wad of cash in Jazzy's hand. "Where did you get all that money?" I demanded. "I hope it's not our rent money. You out here profiling like you one of them Real Housewives."

Mr. Henderson guffawed. "I swear you two haven't changed since Big used to bring you here for ice pops." He shook his head. "Even then you were like fire and ice. Always going at it."

"Yeah. That's because Jazzy was always up to no good. Kind of like how I'm feeling now."

"Would you close your mouth?" Jazzy said, giving me the side-eye. "Not that it's your business but I've been saving money doing hair. I've been fixing heads round the clock and you would've known that if your nose wasn't in them books or your behind at church all the time.

"Don't come for me, Jazzy," I warned.

Mr. Henderson went into another fit of laughter, slapping his hand on the counter. "You girls crack me up."

I stepped back, mindful of the spittle running down the side of his mouth. I wasn't about to get sprayed.

Jazzy met Mr. Henderson's gaze. "I need…" She lowered her voice.

Mr. Henderson stopped laughing. "What did you say?" His eyes narrowed to slits.

My stomach clenched. What had Jazzy said? I leaned forward to catch her words.

"I need a *big bag* of Funyuns," she said.

Is she buying drugs? A ticket to a dog fight? A male prostitute?

"What do you need it for?" Mr. Henderson shot back.

Jazzy lifted her chin, her nose upturned. "Never you mind that. I want to know if you got one or not." Her chest moved in and out while she waited for Mr. Henderson to answer.

Then her true request hit me. I gasped and moved from the counter, shaking my head. "Jazzy, you can't seriously be asking—"

The door creaked and Ms. Miller and her four kids

piled in the store. Jazzy stuffed the cash in her bra. We stood on the side the ten minutes it took Ms. Miller to gather the items and her kids to pay for her stuff. My eyebrows shot up when Jazzy offered to pay for their sodas and treats.

Ms. Miller touched her chest. "Oh, God bless you, child." She sniffed. "I was praying that I could get my chi'ren some snacks and God done come through." She lifted her hands. "Won't he do it?" She eyed Jazzy's cash and said, "I sure wish I had enough to buy some chicken and potatoes."

I rolled my eyes and I could see Jazzy pressing down on her lips to keep from laughing. Ms. Miller was known to be dramatic...and a liar. She most likely wanted, not needed, the money to make a stop at the liquor store.

Jazzy shook her head. "I have to buy Big's medicine."

I chuckled. Ms. Miller had been checked. Jazzy was a better liar than she was.

"All right, child," she said, patting Jazzy's arm. "God bless you and give Big my love. I've been meaning to stop by."

Ms. Miller scooped up her kids and left the store.

"So, you got it?" Jazzy continued.

Mr. Henderson puffed his chest. "You know I got everything. Anything anybody need, I got it." He shuffled past them and headed to the back room. "I'll be back in a jiffy."

Jazzy nodded and shifted her bra, took out the cash, and placed it on the counter.

"Please don't do this," I said to her. "Big wouldn't approve."

"Which is why she won't ever know," Jazzy said. "And you won't be telling her. I've got plans and I'm going to need to protect myself. You have your God and I'll have mine."

I got into her face. "You realize you're no better than Flip and the rest of the hoodrats who use Mr. Henderson for their gun supply." I pointed a finger in her chest. "One of those guns killed our brother, and now you're buying another one?" I shook my head. "I can't believe you." I made a move to leave. "I'm getting out of here."

Jazzy snatched my hand. "No, please don't leave me," she begged. Her lips quivered and her eyes held fear. "I can't do this without you."

My chest heaved. "Then let's go." I grabbed the cash. "Tell Mr. Henderson you changed your mind."

She gave a jerky shake of her head and took her money out of my hands. "I—I have to do this. Before we suspected that it was Flip who killed Jhavon, but now we know for sure. I can't sit back and do nothing. That would make me worse than Sean."

My heart tightened at the mention of his name.

"You should take your sister's advice, Jazzy," Mr. Henderson said, coming back into the room, holding a small box. "Leave it alone."

We both jumped. I don't know how Mr. Henderson could move with such stealth for his age.

He switched his Open sign to Closed and locked the door. When the lock clicked, I felt like I was going to throw up. Jazzy's eyes were wide as well and she grabbed my hand. Her palm was wet and sweaty just like mine. As much as we were at odds about so many things, she was still my twin and I couldn't leave.

Mr. Henderson placed the box on the counter and opened it. Like Pandora, we both leaned in to look into the box.

I released a huge breath.

"It's smaller than I thought," Jazzy said, wiping her brow. "I need something that will do major damage." Her bravado was back but I felt her trembling beside me.

"It's a Colt Mustang XSP. It'll kill just as quick and clean as the next gun. The perfect pistol for you," Mr. Henderson said. He challenged her with a fierce gaze. "You want it?"

Jazzy dropped the cash and picked up the pistol with her fingertips. She didn't know how to hold it, let alone shoot it, which made me all the more antsy. She was more likely to shoot somebody by accident than wipe out Flip.

"You don't want none of Flip and 'em," Mr. Henderson warned, though still counting the cash. "You won't get away with it." He shook his head and studied Jazzy. "I can tell you're not going to listen to me but you should. Thank God Sean listened when I told him not to mention Flip and his crew to the cops."

I furrowed my brow. Jazzy put the gun back in its box. She was all ears as well.

"*You* told Sean not to tell?" I asked.

Mr. Henderson nodded. "Yeah. I heard everything that went down from my window. A lot of stuff happens behind these shops, you know. Mostly fights and other dealings, but I hear 'em. The thing with your brother happened quick." He snapped his fingers. "Sean came through after the shot was fired. He was all bloodied and beat up, but it wasn't from Flip 'cause they'd already left. Sean wanted to call the cops and tell 'em everything. But I knew he'd get himself killed, and that boy had been through enough. What with his father beating him to a pulp that night. I had to take him upstairs and clean him up. I had to pull out my old army medic tools and stitch up his eyebrow.

"I never seen somebody beat so bad still able to move and talk. But he had been determined to make it here for his friend. I had a hard time keeping him quiet from all the crying he did that night." Mr. Henderson shook his head and went to unlock the door. "But when he told me how his Pop beat him, I tell you, I wanted to use one of those on that man myself." Mr. Henderson pointed to the gun. "But I convinced him to say he and Jhavon had been jumped and that he didn't know who fired the shot."

I covered my mouth and placed a hand over my stomach. "He… His *father* beat him?"

"Beat him like he tried to run off the plantation," Mr. Henderson recalled. "That's why he didn't make it in time to have Jhavon's back, 'cause his daddy darn near handicapped him."

What else didn't I know?

My heart pounded in my chest. I placed a hand over my mouth. Oh, my goodness. I had accused Sean of being selfish and a murderer. *What have I done?*

"Yeah," Mr. Henderson said, giving me a weird look as Jazzy and I went through the door. "Didn't you know that? Why else you think he wasn't there that night? I told him to get out of this here town. Leave it all behind—his Pops, the whole thing Flip pulled him and Jhavon into, the memories of what he saw. I don't know why he came back." Mr. Henderson looked at me. "I guess because of you."

I gulped. "Me?"

"Yeah. I've lived a long time, young lady. I know when a male is hankering after a female. And I keep my ear to the ground in Lovetown. But he came by yesterday to tell me he's leaving. Today. Heading to Washington D.C. Good for him. Good for him."

My mouth dropped open. "Sean's leaving? Like leaving for good?" A deep sense of loss filled my heart. I felt like a truck had slammed my insides. I spun around to leave.

"Where you going?" Jazzy grabbed my wrist. "You'd better not be about to tell me you're going to see Sean. He caused our brother's death."

"Then I won't tell you." I jerked free of her grip and scurried away without looking behind. All I could think of was the person ahead whose face I needed to see.

23

THE NIGHT JHAVON DIED...CONTINUED

Sean slid on a pair of sneakers and readied himself to join Jhavon on the other side of the window, when Pop opened Sean's bedroom door and switched on the light.

"What the—" Pop's mouth hung open.

Sean swung around to face his father. Jhavon ducked from sight but not before Pop saw him.

"I knew it." Pop snarled, bunching his fists. "You *are* gay. Sneaking that boy in your room." He made his way toward Sean with fire in his eyes. "That's sick. Disgusting." He struck Sean hard in his face.

"No. No," Jhavon yelled, "Mr. Morr—"

"Get off my property before I put a bullet—"

"Jhavon, go," Sean called. "Don't worry about me, just go."

Sean watched his friend scramble away and felt a sense

of relief. At least they would be off the hook with Flip. He squared his shoulders, preparing himself to face his father, feeling a sense of relief that they would both be off the hook with Flip. Sean was in for another fight with his dad, but at least they weren't going to be killed.

Over the years, the fights with his father had gotten better, if that's what one could call it. Back when he was twelve and Pop had beat him badly, he had almost flunked seventh grade for missing too many days of school. Now that Sean was almost an adult, he could hold his own and keep his father from pulverizing him, putting him in a sleep hold, or giving him a swollen eye.

But tonight was different. The rage at the very idea that Sean was gay and that he and Jhavon had been hiding it in plain sight seemed to give Sean's father another source of energy.

Kicks, blows, and hits came fast and furious, along with cursing and vulgarities. Sean knew he had to stop fighting fair if he wanted to help Jhavon. He picked up a chair and slammed it across his father's back. Pop dropped to the floor and Sean propelled toward the door. But Pop grabbed him by the leg, causing Sean to trip and fall.

That's when Sean went limp. His eyes went wide and he forgot to breathe. There were two

bundles of money under the bed. How could this have happened? How did the money come out of the bag? His heart beat at the speed of a departing train. Was it when he'd thrown it under the bed? Or when he snatched it to throw it out the window?

Sean punched the floor. He had to catch Jhavon before he got to Flip and gave him the bag that did not contain all of his money.

Springing into action, Sean tried to grab the money. Just when it was within reach, he experienced an explosion at the back of his head. Sean staggered from the impact, grabbing his head. His dad had hit him with something. It took him a minute to stand but his arms felt wooden, and his legs wobbled.

"Son, I'll take you out of this world before I watch you destroy our family name," Pop fussed. "You're a *man.*"

Sean tried to speak, but the words he spoke hurt his ears. "You don't understand."

"You're right. I don't understand you people. Just be what *God* made you to be."

Hearing any reference to God coming from such a vile person made Sean nauseous. Or maybe it was the hit to his head. He raced to the toilet and upchucked his stomach contents.

"That's right," Pop said from behind him. "Puke it all up. And go to bed. Wake up in the morning a *man.*" With a maniacal laugh, Pop went back to his room.

Stomach empty, Sean gripped the bowl until he was able to stand. He splashed his face with water and blinked, praying the room would stop spinning.

He closed his eyes. "God, help me," he begged, though he had no relationship with God whatsoever.

Yet God must have listened because when he opened his eyes, the room was still.

Sean crawled under his bed and got the money. The time on his clock was 11:58 p.m. He dove through the window and took off running as fast as he could to Crowley's. Halfway there, Sean had to slow his pace. His eye was swollen shut and his leg throbbed. The adrenaline had worn off and he was aware of every bruise and every chipped bone in his body.

Sean pressed on despite the pain and the near blindness.

But he was too late.

24

NIYA

"Lord, please don't let me be too late," I huffed. Just my luck, I had left my cell phone at home charging. When I was with Jazzy, it hadn't mattered that I didn't have my phone with me. Sweat dripped down my aching body. I hadn't pushed my body like this in years. But I had no other choice. My heels were slowing me down, but I couldn't take them off and risk stepping on broken glass bottles. I couldn't wait to get on the other side of the tracks.

I kept on praying to God while running those blocks from Mr. Henderson's to Sean's place. "God, please help me. Help me," I panted. While running and praying, it occurred to me that Sean must have been running just as fast or faster when he was trying to save Jhavon. Only Sean had been bloodied and battered. His love for Jhavon had pushed him through. And now my love for him would do the same.

Never before was I so glad to live in a small town. I

made it to Sean's apartment complex in twenty-five minutes. His car was parked in the lot.

My heart thumped when I saw a moving truck exiting the complex. I was too late. I was too late. I felt the tears threaten but I waved to Wanda at the front desk and rushed toward the elevator. I pressed the button to Sean's floor. My heart hammered against my chest. I slipped out of my sandals and held them in my hands. I tapped my feet watching the elevator climb to his floor. As soon as the door opened, I rushed toward Sean's apartment. As if on some silent cue, his door opened and out walked Sean with two huge suitcases in tow.

"Sean," I called his name.

He froze, peering at me like he couldn't believe what he was seeing. Then he backed up into the open door. I sprinted toward him before he could close the door.

"Sean." I called again.

He dropped his bags. "Why are you here? I can't be within 50 feet of you and you made it very clear you wanted nothing to do with me. Have you come to get me arrested on my last day in this town?"

"No… I need to speak with you," I breathed out, struggling to catch my breath. "Can I come in?"

Sean took out his cell phone and pressed a button. "Ask me, again. And say your name."

I wanted to be upset at his recording me, but I understood. "This is Janiya. Can I come in?"

With a terse nod, Sean ended the recording and stepped

aside and let me enter his place. I looked around the stark apartment and goosebumps popped up on my arm. If it had been two minutes later, I would've missed him. Missed my chance at happiness. That is if Sean would still have me.

He stormed into the kitchen and returned with a bottle of water. He held it out to me. "I was taking this on the road, but you look like you need it more than me."

I suddenly realized how I must look, hot and sweaty… and tired. "Thank you," I said, taking the bottle from him. "I walked here from Mr. Henderson's."

He lifted a brow. "So he told you I'm leaving. Did you come to gloat then? Is that it?"

I took a couple gulps and wiped my mouth with the back of my hand. "I came to say I'm sorry," I said in a contrite tone. The tears did fall then. They ran down my cheeks. And I let them.

His eyes widened but he squared his shoulders. "Apology accepted." Then he moved toward his suitcases.

My heart screamed. He was leaving me. For good.

"Sean," I cried, clutching my aching chest. "Don't go. Please."

He put a hand on his hip and pinned me with a gaze. "Why should I stay? So you can keep throwing all the love I have for you in my face? There is nothing for me here. You made that plain."

My body convulsed. "Don't leave me, Sean. I'm sorry if I took your love for granted but I was so angry, I thought that… Never mind all that, there is something…well, someone here... Me." I pointed toward my heart. "I love you." Once I had said the words, I knew I had to say them again. "I love you. I love you."

He stood there unmoving before picking up his suitcases. I released a breath of air and my knees buckled.

I had lost him. Now I understood the devastation he must have felt at my rejection. It felt like someone was ripping at the arteries and veins surrounding my heart from my chest. I covered my face and sobbed.

I would've fallen to the floor, if two strong hands didn't catch me. Sean pulled me into a tight embrace. I inhaled his scent, feeling like I had come home.

"I love you too, honey," he said. The timbre of his voice melted my insides. "I never stopped loving you."

My heart flooded as my love multiplied and intensified. We stood there for what seemed like forever. Melding into one another. I felt him shaking and realized he was as overwhelmed as I was. We held onto each other and cried.

Sean pulled away first, loosely holding onto my hand. "Niya, I'm so sorry. I'm sorry I couldn't save Jhavon."

"I know everything, Sean. Mr. Henderson filled me in," I said, placing a finger over his soft lips. "Babe, it wasn't your fault."

"But when I found Jhavon's body on the ground, I tried to—"

"Stop," I said in a firm voice. "Don't. Flip is the one to blame for everything."

He fell silent as I ran my finger along the scar above his

eyebrow. I cocked my head. “Was it your father who gave you this scar?”

He nodded as tears spilled down his cheeks. “I didn’t want anyone to know.”

I lifted my chin. “I’m sorry for what I said to you. About wishing you were dead,” I said. “That was a terrible thing to say.”

He shook his head. “I said it too. I wished it were me instead of Jhavon. He had so much going for him. And he was my friend.”

Sean’s voice broke and he pulled me into him again. He sobbed like...like a man who’d lost his best friend all over again. His wails told me he’d been holding in all this baggage, all this guilt since the night Jhavon died.

I rubbed small circles on his back. “Jhavon’s okay now, Sean. He believed in Jesus,” I said. “He’s fine now.”

Breathing hard, Sean wiped his face, though fresh tears appeared, making the attempt futile. “I know. But it’s just...he didn’t have to die.”

“No. He didn’t die. He’s only sleeping.” My strength surprised me. Here I was looking up into Sean’s face, trying to comfort him rather than the other way around. “God’s got him. We both gotta move on.”

Sean nodded and tilted his head at his luggage by the front door. “That’s what I’m doing. I’m moving to DC. I’m glad we had this closure.”

I gave him a quizzical glance. “You’re moving on.

Without me?" All my hopes plummeted like a huge puddle at my feet.

"God knows I don't want to. We love each other but after everything that's happened...I can understand why you wouldn't trust me or want to—"

I reached up and grabbed the back of his head, pulling him into a hard kiss, erasing all doubt about our future together. "Sean Morrison, I love you. I love you now more than I did before. You were a true friend to my brother, and you've been nothing but good to me. We've both got some bad memories here in Lovetown. I say we move forward. Together."

Sean smiled. "We gotta make some quick moves. You down for a courthouse ceremony? We can stop in North Carolina or Virginia on the way, get the license and get married on the same day."

"In a heartbeat," I replied, though my heart pounded. "I just need a few minutes to pack and to tell Jazzy and Big goodbye."

"All right." He leaned down to kiss me, our second kiss of the day. "I've got a place already. And we'll find you a school in DC. You can transfer your hours and continue working toward your degree."

We left his apartment and headed to his car. Sean put his suitcases in the trunk and then opened the door for me to get inside.

He pulled out of the lot. I thought of Jazzy and Big and

clutched the seat. "My sister and grandmother are going to throw a major fit. I hope you ready for that."

"As long as we're together, I can face the wrath of Zeus himself," Sean said, patting my hand. His confidence gave me the courage I needed.

Sean focused on the road, intertwining his hand in mine.

As he drove, I looked around at the meek surroundings. Wide trees and narrow street lanes. Our one grocery store down the street on the right, a family-owned sno-cone shack to the left. I sniffled. I was going to miss this place.

I gulped. "Will we ever come back here to live?" I asked in a small voice. We were leaving the only home I had ever known.

"I don't know, Niya." He draped an arm across the headrest. I leaned into his arm. "I don't know if there's anything else left that I need from here. I have what I came for." He gave me a pointed look.

I straightened and smiled. "I don't need anything else, either. Just you."

"We'll visit your family, or maybe they will decide to move with us."

I leaned forward, excited at that prospect. "I hope they come and leave this podunk town." In a flash, all sorts of visions filled my mind. "Jazzy could expand and get more clients. And Big would get better care."

Sean pulled over by Mr. Henderson's and looked at me. "Baby, they might not decide to come. I know you're going to miss your twin sister, especially since you've never been away from each other. Will I be enough for you?"

I chewed on my lower lip, pondering his question before facing Sean.

I saw the vulnerability in his eyes and all my fears dissipated. I stretched up to kiss him on the cheek. "Yes, honey, I'll be fine. Even if they don't come. I'll be all right because I have you. These weeks of living without you were torture. I'm not saying I wouldn't survive but being with you gives my life a whole other level of meaning."

"I feel the same way about you." He smiled. Tenderness shone from his eyes. "We will be okay."

He got back on the road. I closed my eyes and smiled. We would be more than okay. We were together. That's all that mattered.

DISCUSSION QUESTIONS

1. Big said that their family had a "hex" on them; they died young. At first, Niya believed that prophesy. How do you handle it when people say bad things about your destiny?
2. Sean fears he won't be a good father because he didn't have a good father. Do you think this is a valid concern? How can a parent learn the skills they need despite never having experienced good parenting?
3. Discuss how Niya's character changed from the beginning of the story until the end. What are some of the feelings she experienced and how did she overcome them?
4. Sean suffered verbal and physical abuse from his father yet he didn't tell. Why do you think he didn't talk about it? What are some of the classic

signs of someone who has been abused? What advice can you give to someone in this situation?

5. What are some ways in which Sean's relationship with God guided his life? He didn't always do what God would do, but do you think his love for God was genuine? Are there times in your life where you are not willing or ready to follow God's leading? What is holding you back, and how can you move forward?
6. We can see from Jazzy's attitude at the end of the story that she is unwilling to forgive Sean for her brother's death. Do you agree with her or do you understand her position?
7. How would you define Jazzy and Niya's relationship? As twins they share a special bond. Do you think that needs to change now that Niya is with Sean?

ABOUT THE AUTHORS

Michelle Lindo-Rice

Michelle Lindo-Rice is the Bestselling Author of the "Able to Love" and "On The Right Path" series. She enjoys crafting fiction centered around the four "F" words: Faith, Friendship, Family, and Forgiveness. Michelle is the 2015 winner of the Black Writers And Book Clubs Rocks Female Author of the Year Award. Originally from Jamaica West Indies, she views herself as a lifelong learner. She has earned degrees from New York University, SUNY at Stony Brook, Teachers College Columbia University and Argosy University. A pastor's kid, Michelle upholds the faith, preaching, teaching, and ministering through praise and worship.

Join Michelle Lindo-Rice's mailing list (http://bit.ly/2rLVEUJ) to keep up with her latest releases and upcoming projects.

* * *

Michelle Stimpson

Bestselling author Michelle Stimpson has penned more than fifty faith-based books including traditional bestseller *Boaz Brown,* the beloved Mama B series, and *Deacon Brown's Daughter's*, for which she produced an award-winning independent film. Additionally, she has published more than fifty short stories through her educational publishing company, WeGottaRead.com. Michelle holds an English degree from

Jarvis Christian College and a master's degree in education from the University of Texas at Arlington. She loves combining her passion for writing with her gift of teaching in various capacities.

Join Michelle's email list (http://bit.ly/2QiQD0e) and receive notice of new books and contests and to keep in touch!